ETCHED IN MOONLIGHT

Etched
in Moonlight

By
James Stephens

New York

The Macmillan Company

1928

SET UP BY BROWN BROTHERS, LINOTYPERS
PRINTED IN THE UNITED STATES OF AMERICA
BY THE CORNWALL PRESS

CONTENTS

DESIRE

ETCHED IN MOONLIGHT

DESIRE

I

HE was excited, and as he leaned forward in his chair and told this story to his wife he revealed to her a degree or a species of credulity of which she could not have believed him capable.

He was a level-headed man, and habitually conducted his affairs on hard-headed principles. IIe had conducted his courtship, his matrimonial and domestic affairs in a manner which she should not have termed reckless or romantic. When, therefore, she found him excited, and over such a story, she did not know how just to take the matter.

She compromised by agreeing with him, not because her reason was satisfied or even touched, but simply because he was excited, and a woman can welcome anything which varies the dull round and will bathe in exclamations if she gets the chance.

This was what he told her.

As he was walking to lunch a motor car came down the street at a speed much too dangerous for the narrow and congested thoroughfare. A man was walking in front of him, and, just as the car came behind, this man stepped off the path with a view to crossing the road. He did not even look behind as he stepped off. Her husband stretched a ready arm that swept the man back to the pavement one second before the car went blaring and buzzing by.

"If I had not been there," said her husband, who liked slang, "you would have got it where the chicken got the axe."

The two men grinned at each other; her husband smiling with good-fellowship, the other crinkling with amusement and gratitude.

They walked down the street and, on the strength of that adventure, they had lunch together.

They had sat for a long time after lunch,

making each other's acquaintance, smoking innumerable cigarettes, and engaged in a conversation which she could never have believed her husband would have shared in for ten minutes; and they had parted with a wish, from her husband, that they should meet again on the following day, and a wordless smile from the man.

He had neither ratified nor negatived the arrangement.

"I hope he'll turn up," said her husband.

This conversation had excited her man, for it had drawn him into an atmosphere to which he was a stranger, and he had found himself moving there with such pleasure that he wished to get back to it with as little delay as possible.

Briefly, as he explained it to her, the atmosphere was religious; and while it was entirely intellectual it was more heady and exhilarating than the emotional religion to which he had been accustomed, and from which he had silently lapsed.

He tried to describe his companion; but had such ill success in the description that she could not remember afterwards whether he was tall or short; fat or thin; fair or dark.

It was the man's eyes only that he succeeded in emphasising; and these, it appeared, were eyes such as he had never before seen in a human face.

That also, he amended, was a wrong way of putting it, for his eyes were exactly like everybody else's. It was the way he looked through them that was different. Something, very steady, very ardent, very quiet and powerful, was using these eyes for purposes of vision. He had never met any-one who looked at him so . . . compre-hendingly; so agreeably.

"You are in love," said she with a laugh.

After this her husband's explanations became more explanatory but not less con-fused, until she found that they were both, with curious unconsciousness, in the middle of a fairy-tale.

"He asked me," said her husband," what was the thing I wished for beyond all things.

"That was the most difficult question I have ever been invited to answer," he went on; "and for nearly half an hour we sat thinking it out, and discussing magnificences and possibilities.

"I had all the usual thoughts; and, of course, the first of them was wealth. We are more dominated by proverbial phrases than we conceive of, and, such a question being posed, the words 'healthy, wealthy, and wise' will come, unbidden, to answer it. To be alive is to be acquisitive, and so I mentioned wealth, tentatively, as a possibility; and he agreed that it was worth considering. But after a while I knew that I did not want money."

"One always has need of money," said his wife.

"In a way, that is true," he replied, "but not in this way; for, as I thought it over, I remembered that we have no children; and that our relatively few desires, or fancies, can be readily satisfied by the money we already have. Also we are fairly well off; we have enough in the stocking to last our time even if I ceased from business, which I am not going to do; and, in short, I discovered that money or its purchasing power had not any particular advantages to offer."

"All the same!" she murmured; and halted with her eyes fixed on purchasings far away in time and space.

"All the same!" he agreed with a smile.

"I could not think of anything worth wishing for," he continued. "I mentioned health and wisdom, and we considered these; but, judging myself by the standard of the world in which we move, I concluded that both my health and knowledge were as good as the next man's; and I thought also that if I elected to become wiser than my contemporaries I might be a very lonely person for the rest of my days."

"Yes," said she thoughtfully, "I am glad you did not ask to be made wise, unless you could have asked it for both of us."

"I asked him in the end what he would advise me to demand, but he replied that he could not advise me at all. 'Behind everything stands desire,' said he, 'and you must find out your desire.'

"I asked him then, if the conditions were reversed and if the opportunity had come to him instead of to me, what he should have asked for; not, as I explained to him, in order that I might copy his wish, but from sheer curiosity. He replied that he should not ask for anything. This reply astonished, almost alarmed me at first, but most curiously satisfied me on considering it, and I was about to adopt that attitude——"

"Oh," said his wife.

"When an idea came to me. 'Here I am,' I said to myself, 'forty-eight years of age: rich enough; sound enough in wind and limb; and as wise as I can afford to be. What is there now belonging to me, absolutely mine, but from which I must part, and which I should like to keep?' And I saw that the thing which was leaving me day by day; second by second; irretrievably and inevitably; was my forty-eighth year. I thought I should like to continue at the age of forty-eight until my time was up.

"I did not ask to live for ever, or any of that nonsense, for I saw that to live for ever is to be condemned to a misery of boredom more dreadful than anything else the mind can conceive of. But, while I do live, I wish to live competently, and so I asked to be allowed to stay at the age of forty-eight years with all the equipment of my present state unimpaired."

"You should not have asked for such a thing," said his wife, a little angrily. "It is not fair to me," she explained. "You are older than I am now, but in a few years this will mean that I shall be needlessly older than you. I think it was not a loyal wish."

"I thought of that objection," said he, "and I also thought that I was past the age at which certain things matter; and that both temperamentally and in the matter of years I am proof against sensual or such-like attractions. It seemed to me to be right; so I just registered my wish with him."

"What did he say?" she queried.

"He did not say anything; he just nodded; and began to talk again of other matters—religion, life, death, mind; a host of things, which, for all the diversity they seem to have when I enumerate them, were yet one single theme.

"I feel a more contented man to-night than I have ever felt," he continued, "and I feel in some curious way a different person from the man I was yesterday."

Here his wife awakened from the conversation and began to laugh.

[10]

"You are a foolish man," said she, "and I am just as bad. If anyone were to hear us talking this solemn silliness they would have a right to mock at us."

He laughed heartily with her, and after a light supper they went to bed.

II

DURING the night his wife had a dream.

She dreamed that a ship set away for the Polar Seas on an expedition in which she was not sufficiently interested to find out its reason. The ship departed with her on board. All that she knew or cared was that she was greatly concerned with baggage, and with counting and going over the various articles that she had brought against arctic weather.

She had thick woollen stockings. She had skin boots all hairy inside, all pliable and wrinkled without. She had a great skin cap shaped like a helmet and fitting down in a cape over her shoulders. She had, and they did not astonish her, a pair of very baggy fur trousers. She had a sleeping sack.

She had an enormous quantity of things;

and everybody in the expedition was equipped, if not with the same things, at least similarly.

These traps were a continuous subject of conversation aboard, and, although days and weeks passed, the talk of the ship hovered about and fell continually into the subject of warm clothing.

There came a day when the weather was perceptibly colder; so cold that she was tempted to draw on these wonderful breeches, and to fit her head into that most comfortable hat. But she did not do so; for, and everybody on the ship explained it to her, it was necessary that she should accustom herself to the feeling, the experience, of cold; and, she was further assured, that the chill which she was now resenting was nothing to the freezing she should presently have to bear.

It seemed good advice; and she decided that as long as she could bear the cold she would do so, and would not put on any protective covering; thus, when the cold became really intense, she would be in some measure inured to it, and would not suffer so much.

[13]

But steadily, and day by day, the weather grew colder.

For now they were in wild and whirling seas wherein great green and white icebergs went sailing by; and all about the ship little hummocks of ice bobbed and surged, and went under and came up; and the grey water slashed and hissed against and on top of these small hillocks.

Her hands were so cold that she had to put them under her armpits to keep any warmth in them; and her feet were in a worse condition. They had begun to pain her; so she decided that on the morrow she would put on her winter equipment, and would not mind what anybody said to the contrary.

"It is cold enough," said she, "for my arctic trousers, for my warm soft boots, and my great furry gloves. I will put them on in the morning," for it was then almost night and she meant to go to bed at once.

She did go to bed; and she lay there in a very misery of cold.

In the morning, she was yet colder; and immediately on rising she looked for the winter clothing which she had laid ready by

the side of her bunk the night before; but
she could not find them. She was forced to
dress in her usual rather thin clothes; and,
having done so, she went on deck.

When she got to the side of the vessel she
found that the world about her had changed.

The sea had disappeared. Far as the eye
could peer was a level plain of ice, not white,
but dull grey; and over it there lowered a
sky, grey as itself and of almost the same
dullness.

Across this waste there blew a bitter, a
piercing wind that her eyes winced from,
and that caused her ears to tingle and
sting.

Not a soul was moving on the ship, and
the dead silence which brooded on the ice
lay heavy and almost solid on the vessel.

She ran to the other side, and found that
the whole ship's company had landed, and
were staring at her from a little distance off
the ship. And these people were as silent
as the frozen air, as the frozen ship. They
stared at her; they made no move; they
made no sound.

She noticed that they were all dressed in

their winter furs; and, while she stood, ice began to creep into her veins.

One of the ship's company strode forward a few paces and held up a bundle in his mittened hand. She was amazed to see that the bundle contained her clothes; her broad furry trousers; her great cosy helmet and gloves.

To get from the ship to the ice was painful but not impossible. A rope ladder was hanging against the side, and she went down this. The rungs felt hard as iron, for they were frozen stiff; and the touch of those glassy surfaces bit into her tender hand like fire. But she got to the ice and went across it towards her companions.

Then, to her dismay, to her terror, all these, suddenly, with one unexpressed accord, turned and began to run away from her; and she, with a heart that shook once and could scarcely beat again, took after them.

Every few paces she fell, for her shoes could not grip on the ice; and each time that she fell those monsters stood and turned and watched her, and the man who had her clothes waved the bundle at her and danced grotesquely, silently.

She continued running, sliding, falling, picking herself up, until her breath went, and she came to a halt, unable to move a limb further and scarcely able to breathe; and this time they did not stay to look at her.

They continued running, but now with great and greater speed, with the very speed of madmen; and she saw them become black specks away on the white distance; and she saw them disappear; and she saw that there was nothing where she stared but the long white miles, and the terrible silence, and the cold.

How cold it was!

And with that there arose a noiseless wind, keen as a razor.

It stung into her face; it swirled about her ankles like a lash; it stabbed under her armpits like a dagger.

"I am cold," she murmured.

She looked backwards whence she had come, but the ship was no longer in sight, and she could not remember from what direction she had come.

Then she began to run in any direction.

Indeed she ran in every direction to find

the ship; for when she had taken an hundred steps in one way she thought, frantically, "this is not the way," and at once she began to run on the opposite road. But run as she might she could not get warm; it was colder she got. And then, on a steel-grey plane, she slipped, and slipped again, and went sliding down a hollow, faster and faster; she came to the brink of a cleft, and swished over this, and down into a hole of ice and there she lay.

"I shall die!" she said. "I shall fall asleep here and die. . . ."

Then she awakened.

She opened her eyes directly on the window and saw the ghost of dawn struggling with the ghoul of darkness. A greyish perceptibility framed the window without, but could not daunt the obscurity within; and she lay for a moment terrified at that grotesque adventure, and thanking God that it had only been a dream.

In another second she felt that she was cold. She pulled the clothes more tightly about her, and she spoke to her husband.

"How miserably cold it is!" she said.

She turned in the bed and snuggled against him for warmth; and she found that an atrocity of cold came from him; that he was icy.

She leaped from the bed with a scream. She switched on the light, and bent over her husband—

He was stone dead. He was stone cold. And she stood by him, shivering and whimpering.

HUNGER

TO
W. T. H. HOWE

HUNGER

I

ON some people misery comes unrelentingly. It comes with such a continuous rage that one might say destruction had been sworn against them and that they were doomed beyond appeal, or hope.

'That seemed to her to be the case as she sat, when her visitor had departed, looking on life as it had moved about her; and she saw that life had closed on her, had crushed her, and that there was nothing to be said about it, and no one to be blamed.

She was ten years married, and she had three children. One of them had fallen when he was a baby, and had hurt his back so badly that the dispensary doctor instructed her not to let him walk for a few years.

She loved all her children, but this child

she loved greatly; for she had to do more for him than for the others. Indeed she had to do everything for him, and she did not grudge doing it. He was the eldest and he was always with her. The other youngsters were with her as screamings, as demands, to be attended to and forgotten, but he was with her as a companion eye, a consciousness to whom she could talk and who would reply to her, and who would not, could not, by any means get into mischief.

Her husband was a house-painter, and when work was brisk he got good wages: he could earn thirty-five shillings a week when he was working.

But his work was constant only in the summer months: through the bad weather there was no call for him, for no one wanted house-painting done in the winter; and so the money which he earned in the fine months had to be stretched and made to cover the dead months.

Nor were these five months to be entirely depended upon: here and there in a week days would be missed, and with that his Society dues had to be paid, for he would pay these though he starved for it.

[24]

II

Wages which have to be stretched so
lengthily give but the slenderest sum towards
a weekly budget. It was she who had to
stretch them, and the doing of it occupied
all the time she could spare for thinking.

She made ends meet where nothing was
but ends, and they met just over the starvation line.

She had not known for years what it was
like not to be hungry for one day; but life
is largely custom; and neither she nor her
husband nor the children made much complaint about a condition which was normal
for them all, and into which the children had
been born.

They could scarcely die of hunger for
they were native to it. They were hunger.
There was no other hunger but them: and

they only made a noise about food when they saw food.

If she could have got work how gladly she would have taken it! How gladly she would have done it! Sweated work! Any work! so it brought in if it was no more than a few coppers in the day. But the children were there, three of them, and all were young and one was a cripple.

Her own people, and those of her husband, lived, existed, far away in the country. They could not take the children off her hands. She could not give a neighbour anything to look after them while she went out working. She was held to them as fast as if she were chained to them; and, for to think in such cases is only to be worried, there was no use in thinking about it. She had already all the work she could deal with, and she wanted no more.

She remembered a tale that she had laughed at, when she was young, about a woman who had been circumstanced as she was now. This woman used to put her two children into a box, for she had to go out every day to work in order that she might feed them; and she kept them in the box so that they might not injure themselves during her absence.

It was a good idea, but the children came out of the box hunchbacks, and so stunted in their growth that it might be said they never grew thereafter. It might have been better for the children, and easier for them, if they had died; anyhow, their mother died, and the poor little oddities went to the work-house; and must all their lives have got all the jeers which their appearance sanctioned.

There was nothing to be done; even her husband had long ago given up thinking of how this could be arranged; and although she still, and continually, thought about it, she knew that nothing could be done.

III

HER husband was a jolly man; he used to make up lists of the gigantic feeds they would have when the ship came home (what ship he did not say, nor was it understood that he expected one), and he or she or the children would remind each other of foods which had been left out of his catalogue; for no food of which they knew the name could justly be omitted from their future.

He was a robust man, and could have eaten a lot had he got it. Indeed he had often tempted his wife to commit an act of madness and have one wild blow-out; for which, as she pointed out to him, they would have to pay by whole days of whole starvation, instead of the whole days of semi-hunger to which they were accustomed.

This was the only subject on which they

came nigh to quarrelling, and he brought it
forward with fortnightly regularity.

Sometimes she went cold at the thought
that on some pay-day he might go in for a
wild orgy of eating, and perhaps spend half
a crown. Less than that sum could not
nearly fill him; and the double of it would
hardly fill him the way he needed to be filled;
for he wanted to be filled as tightly as a
drum, and with such a weight and abundance
of victual that he could scarcely be lifted by
a crane.

But he was an honourable man, and she
knew that he would not do this unless she
and the children were with him and could
share and go mad with him. He was very
fond of them, and if she could have fed him
on her own flesh she would have sacrificed a
slice or two, for she was very fond of him.

IV

THE mild weather had come, and he got a cut in his hand, which festered and seemed stubbornly incurable. The reason was that the gaunt man was not fed well enough to send clean blood down to doctor his cut hand. In the end he did get over it; but for three weeks he had been unable to work, for who will give employment to a man whose hand looks like a poultice or a small football?

The loss of these three weeks almost finished her.

The distinguishing mark of her family had been thinness, it was now bonyness.

To what a food-getting fervour was she compelled! She put the world of rubbish that was about her through a sieve; and winnowed nourishment for her family where a rat would have unearthed disappointment.

She could not beg; but she did send her two children into the street, and sometimes one of these got a copper from a passing stranger. Then, like the call of a famished crow who warns his brothers that he has discovered booty, that youngster gave out a loyal squeal for his companion; and they trotted home with their penny. The sun shone on the day they got a penny; on the days when they got nothing the sun might bubble the tar and split the bricks, but it did not shine.

Her man returned to his work, and if she could hold on they would be able to regain the poverty of a few months previously, but which now beamed to her as distant, unattainable affluence.

She could hold on, and she did; so that they tided feebly across those evil days; and came nigh at last to the longed-for scarcity which yet was not absolute starvation; and whereby they could live in the condition of health to which they were accustomed, and which they recognised and spoke of as good health.

They could not absolutely come to this for at least a year. Provision had still to be made for the lean months to come; the winter months; and more than three weeks' wages which should have been skimmed in this precaution had been unprofitable, had not existed. The difference had to be made up by a double skimming of the present wage; which must also pay the present necessities, and recoup the baker and grocer for the few weeks' credit these shop people had given her.

In all, their lot for a long time was not to be envied, except by a beast in captivity: and envied only by him because he lusts for freedom and the chance of it as we lust for security and the destruction of chance.

V

THE winter came—the winter will come tho'
the lark protest and the worm cries out its
woe—and she entered on that period with
misgiving, with resolution, and with a facing
of everything that might come.

What bravery she had! What a noble,
unwearying courage; when in so little a time,
and at so small a pain, she might have died!

But such an idea did not come to her
head. She looked on the world, and she
saw that it was composed of a man and three
children; while they lasted she could last,
and when they were done it would be time
enough to think of personal matters and
her relation to things.

Before the summer had quite ended, e'er
autumn had tinted a leaf, the war broke out;
and with its coming there came insecurity.

Not to her, not to them. They had no standard to measure security by. It came to the people who desire things done, and who pay to have doors varnished or window-frames painted. These people drew silently but resolutely from expense; while he and she and the children sunk deeper into their spending as one wallows into a bog.

The prices of things began to increase with a cumulative rapidity, and the quality of things began to deteriorate with equal speed. Bread and the eater of it came to a grey complexion. Meat was no more. The vegetables emigrated with the birds. The potato got a rise in the world and recognised no more its oldest friends. Nothing was left but the rain; and the rain came loyally.

They, those others, could retrench and draw in a little their horns; but from what could she retreat? What could she avoid? What could she eliminate, who had come to the bare bone and shank of life? The necessity for the loaf comes daily, recurs pitilessly from digestion to digestion, and with the inexorable promptitude of the moon the rent collector wanes and waxes.

They managed.

She and he managed.

Work still was, although it was spaced and intervalled like a storm-blown hedge. Here was a week and there another one, and from it they gleaned their constricted existence.

They did not complain; for those who are down do not complain. Nor did they know they were down. Or, knowing it, they did not admit their downness. For to front so final a fact is to face with naked hands a lion; and to admit is to give in. Is to be washed away. To be lost and drowned. To be anonymous; unhelpable; alive no more; but débris, or a straw which the wind takes and sails, or tears, or drifts, or rots, to powder and forgetfulness.

A bone in a world of bones! And they gnawed these bones until it seemed that nothing moved in the world except their teeth.

VI

THE winter came, and his work stopped as it always did in that season.

He got jobs cleaning windows. He got jobs at the docks hoisting things which not Hercules nor the devil himself could lift. But which he could lift, or which his teeth and the teeth of his children detached from the ground as from foundations and rivettings.

He got a job as a coalman; and as a night-watchman sitting in the angle of a black street before a bucket of stinking coal, which had been a fire until the rain put it out. To-day he had a job; but to-morrow and for a week he had none.

With what had been saved, skimmed, strained from the summer wages; with what came from the jobs; with the pennies that the children unearthed from strangers as though they dug in those loath souls for coin, they lived through the winter, and did not feel that they had passed through an experience worthy of record, or that their endurance might have been rewarded with medals and a pension.

They were living, as we all manage, amazingly, to live: and if others had an easier time that was their chance. But this was their life, and there were those who were even worse off than they were.

For they paid the rent! And, when that was done, what a deed had been accomplished! How notable an enemy circumvented!

VII

THE spring came; but it brought no leaves to their tree. The summer came; but it did not come to them; nor warn them of harvest and a sickle in the yield.

There was no building done that summer; the price of material had gone up and the price of wages. The contractors did not care for that prospect, and the client, remembering taxes and the war, decided to wait.

And her husband had no work!

Almost he had even given up looking for work. He would go out of the house and come into the house and go out of the house again; and he and she would look at each other in a dumb questioning.

It was strange how he had arranged with himself not to look at the children. How he had even arranged that their whimperings should seem to be inaudible, and their very presences invisible! And they, having raked his coming as with search-lights, and discovering that he brought nothing, looked at him no more.

They looked at her. They projected themselves to her, about her, upon her, into her. . . .

A wolf-mother, thus badgered and possessed, would have escaped from her young by mercifully or unmercifully slaughtering them. But she still could preserve her soul, her tenderness. Yet, if a whole infinity of tenderness seemed to be preserved for the children, a major, a yet more marvellous, tenderness was reserved for her man—it was without words, without action. It was without anything whatever. It was itself alone. Unproven, unquestioned, unending. To be perceived, received, only by the soul, and from the soul, or not to be received or perceived at all.

Sometimes she would say—not that she had anything to say, but to ease her husband's heart with a comradely word—

"Any chance to-day, do you think?"

And he would reply:

"Chance!"

And he would sit down to brood upon that lapsing word.

They were not angry; they had not the blood to be angry with; for to be wrathful you must be well fed or you must be drunk.

The youngest child died of an ill which, whatever it was at the top, was hunger at the bottom; and she grew terrified. She heard that there was work to be had in the Munition Factories in Scotland, and by some means she gathered together the fare and sent her husband across the sea.

"Write, if you can," said she, "the minute you get a place."

"Yes," he replied.

"And send us what you can spare," she said. "Send something this week if you can."

"Yes," he said.

And he went away.

And she went into the streets to beg.

VIII

She left the boy behind in his chair, and brought the other little one with her.

She was frightened, for one can be arrested for begging. And she was afraid not to beg, for one can die of hunger.

How well she knew those streets! and yet she did not know them in this aspect! These were atrocious streets!

She got a penny here and a penny there, and she bought bread. Sometimes even she bought a twist of tea. She could manage until the end of the week; until her man sent the money.

She had thoughts of singing at the corners of streets, as she had so often seen done by the toneless, ashen-faced women, who creak rusty music at the passer, and fix him with their eyes. But she was ashamed; and no song that she could remember seemed suitable; and she only could remember bits of songs; and she knew that her voice would not work for her, but that it would creak and mourn like a rusty hinge.

Her earnings were small, for she could not get in touch with people. That too is a trade and must be learned. They recognised her at a distance as a beggar, and she could only whisper to the back of a head or a cold shoulder.

Sometimes when she went towards a person that person instantly crossed the road and walked for a while hastily.

Sometimes people fixed upon her a prohibitive eye and she drew back from them humbled; her heart panting and her eyes hot at the idea that they took her for a beggar.

At times a man, without glancing at her, stuck a hand in his pocket and gave her a penny without halting in his stride.

One day she got twopence; one day she got sixpence; one day she got nothing.

But she could hold out to the end of the week.

IX

THE end of the week came, but it brought no letter.

"It will come to-morrow," she said.

"He is in a strange country," she thought in panic. "He must have missed the post, God help him!"

But on the next day there was no letter; nor any letter on the day after; and on the day that succeeded to it there was no letter.

"He . . . !" she said.

But she could not speculate on him. She knew him too well, and she knew that this was not he; he could no more leave them in the lurch than he could jump across Ireland in one jump.

"He has not got work," she said.

And she saw him strayed and stranded; without a hand; without a voice; bewildered and lost among strangers; going up streets and down streets; and twisting himself into a maze, a dizziness of loneliness and hunger ·and despair.

Or, she said:

"The submarines had blown up the ship that was coming with the money."

The week went by; another came, and still she did not hear from him. She was not able to pay the rent.

She looked at the children; and then she looked away from them distantly to her strayed husband; and then she looked inwardly on herself, and there was nothing to see.

She was down.

No littlest hope could find a chink to peer through. And while she sat, staring at nothing, in an immobile maze of attention, her mind—she had no longer a heart, it had died of starvation—her mind would give a leap and be still; and would leap again, as though an unknown, wordless action were seeking to be free; seeking to do something; seeking to disprove stagnation, and powerlessness, and death; and a little burning centre of violence hung in her head like a star.

She followed people with her eyes, sometimes a little way with her feet, saying to herself:

"The pockets of that man are full of money; he would rattle if he fell."

Or:

"That man had his breakfast this morning; he is full of food to the chin; he is round and tight and solid, and he weighs a ton."

She said:

"If I had all the money of all the people in this street I should have a lot of money."

She said:

"If I owned all the houses in this street I should have a lot of money."

The rent collector told her imperatively that she must leave at the end of the week, and the children called to her for bread, clamorously, unceasingly, like little dogs that yap and whine and cannot be made to stop.

X

RELIEF kitchens had been started in various parts of the city, but she only heard of them by chance; and she went to one. She told a lady in attendance her miserable tale, and was given the address of a gentleman who might assist her. He could give her a ticket which would enable her to get food; and he might be able to set her in the way of earning what would pay the rent.

This lady thought her husband had deserted her; and she said so, without condemnation, as one states a thing which has been known to happen; and the poor woman agreed without agreeing, for she did not believe it.

But she did not argue about the matter, for now that she accepted food, she accepted anything that came with it, whether it was opinions or advice. She was an acceptor, and if she claimed to possess even an opinion it might jeopardise her chance of getting anything.

She set out for the house of the gentleman who could give her the ticket which would get her food to bring home to the children.

He lived at some distance, and when she got to his house the servant told her he had gone to his office; at his office she was informed that he had gone out. She called three times at the office, and on the third time she was told that he had come in, but had gone home.

She trudged to his house again; and would have been weary, but that her mind had lasped far, far, from her trudging feet; and when the mind is away the body matters nothing.

Where was her mind? At times it was nowhere. It was gone from her body and from material things. It might be said to have utterly quitted that tenement, and to be somehow, somewhere, refuged from every fear, havened from every torment and eased of every memory that could deject it. She was life and a will; or, if these are but one, she was the will to be, obscure, diligent, indefatigable.

And then, again, as at the opening of a door, her mind, laden with recollections of time and space, of deeds and things and thwartings, was back in the known and incredible room, looking at the children, listening to them, consoling them; telling them that in a little while she should be home again, and that she would bring them food.

They had not eaten anything for—how long was it? Was it a year? Had they ever eaten? And one of them was sick!

She must get back. She had been away too long. But she must go forward before she could go back.

She must get the ticket which was food and hope and a new beginning, or a respite. Then she should be able to look about her. The children would go to sleep; and she could plan and contrive and pull together those separated and dwindling ends.

She came to the gentleman's house. He was in, and she told him her story, and how her case was desperate.

He also believed that her husband had deserted her; and he promised to write by that night's post to find out the truth about the man, and to see that he was punished for his desertion.

He had no tickets with him; he had used them all, for the hungry people in Dublin were numerous; work was slack everywhere, and those who had never before applied for assistance were now obliged to do so by dreadful necessity. He gave her some money, and promised to call at her room on the following day to investigate her case.

She went homewards urgently, and near home she bought bread and tea.

When she got in the crippled boy turned dull, dumb eyes upon her; and she laughed at him excitedly, exultantly; for she had food; lots of it, two loaves of it.

But the other child did not turn to her, and would not turn to her again, for he was dead; and he was dead of hunger.

XI

SHE could not afford to go mad, for she still had a boy, and he depended on her with an utter helpless dependence.

She fed him and fed herself; running from him in the chair to that other in its cot, with the dumb agony of an animal who must do two things at once, and cannot resolve which thing to do.

She could not think; she could hardly feel. She was dulled and distressed and wild. She was weakened by misery and tormented by duties; and life and the world seemed a place of busynesses, and futilities, and unending, unregulated, demands upon her.

A neighbour, hearing that persistent trotting over her head, came up to the room to remonstrate, and remained to shed for her the tears which she could not weep herself.

She, too, was in straits, and had nothing more to give than those tears; and the banal iterations which are comfort because they are kindness.

Into this place the gentleman called on the following day to investigate, and was introduced to a room swept almost as clean of furniture as a dog kennel is; to the staring, wise-eyed child who lived in a chair; and to the quiet morsel of death that lay in a cot by the wall.

He was horrified, but he was used to sights of misery; and he knew that when things have ceased to move they must be set moving again; and that all he could do was to remove some of the impediments which he found in the path of life, so that it might flow on before it had time to become stagnant and rotten.

He took from the dry-eyed, tongue-tied woman all the immediate worry of death. He paid the rent, and left something to go on with as well; and he promised to get her work either in his house or at his office, but he would get her work to do somehow.

XII

HE came daily; and each day, in reply to her timid question as to her husband, he had nothing to say except that enquiries were being made.

On the fifth day he had news, and he would have preferred any duty, however painful, to the duty of telling her his news.

But he told it, sitting on the one chair; with his hand over his eyes, and nothing of his face visible except the mouth which shaped and spoke sentences.

The munition people in Scotland reported that a man of the name he was enquiring for had applied for work, and had been taken on a fortnight after his application. The morning after he began work he was found dead in a laneway. He had no lodgings in the city; and at the post-mortem examination it was found that he had died of hunger and exposure.

She listened to that tale; looking from the gentleman who told it to her little son who listened to it. She moistened her lips with her tongue; but she could not speak, she could only stammer and smile.

The gentleman also sat looking at the boy.

"We must set this young man up," said he heavily. "I shall send a doctor to look him over to-day."

And he went away all hot and cold; beating his hands together as he walked; and feeling upon his shoulders all the weariness and misery of the world.

SCHOOLFELLOWS

SCHOOLFELLOWS

I

WE had been at school together and I remembered him perfectly well, for he had been a clever and prominent boy. He won prizes for being at the top of his class; and prizes for good behaviour; and prizes for games. Whatever prizes were going we knew that he should get them; and, although he was pleasant about it, he knew it himself.

He saw me first, and he shouted and waved his hat, but I had jumped on a tram already in motion. He ran after me for quite a distance; but the trams only stop at regular places, and he could not keep up: he fell behind, and was soon left far behind.

I had intended jumping off to shake his hand; but I thought, so fast did he run, that he would catch up; and then the tram went quicker and quicker; and quite a stream of cars and taxis were in the way; so that when the tram did stop he was out of sight. Also I was in a hurry to get home.

Going home I marvelled for a few moments that he should have run so hard after me. He ran almost—desperately.

"It would strain every ounce of a man's strength to run like that!" I said.

And his eyes had glared as he ran!

"Poor old chap!" I thought. "He must have wanted to speak to me very badly."

Three or four days afterwards I met him again; and we talked together for a while on the footpath. Then, at whose suggestion I do not remember, we moved into the bar of an hotel near by.

We drank several glasses of something; for which, noticing that his hat was crumpled and his coat sleeves shiny, I paid. We spoke of the old days at school and he told me of men whom he had met, but whom I had not heard of for a long time. Such old school-fellows as I did know of I mentioned, and in every instance he took their addresses down on a piece of paper.

He asked what I was doing and how I was succeeding and where I lived; and this latter information he pencilled also on his piece of paper.

"My memory is getting bad," he said with a smile.

Every few minutes he murmured into our schoolday conversation—

"Whew! Isn't it hot!"

And at other times, laughing a little, apologising a little, he said:

"I am terribly thirsty to-day; it's the heat, I suppose."

I had not noticed that it was particularly hot; but we are as different in our skins as we are in our souls, and one man's heat may be tepid enough to his neighbour.

II

THEN I met him frequently. One goes home usually at the same hour and by the same road; and it was on these home-goings and on this beaten track that we met.

Somehow, but by what subtle machinery I cannot recall, we always elbowed one another into a bar; and, as his hat was not getting less crumpled nor his coat less shiny, I paid for whatever liquor was consumed.

One can do anything for a long time without noticing it, and the paying for a few drinks is not likely to weigh on the memory. Still, we end by noticing everything; and perhaps I noticed it the earlier because liquor does not agree with me. I never mentioned that fact to anyone, being slightly ashamed of it, but I knew it very woefully myself by the indigestion which for two or three days followed on even a modest consumption of alcohol.

So it was that setting homeward one evening on the habitual track I turned very deliberately from it; and, with the slightest feeling of irritation, I went homewards by another route: and each night that followed I took this new path.

I did not see him for some weeks, and then one evening he hailed me on the new road. When I turned at the call and saw him running—he was running—I was annoyed, and, as we shook hands, I became aware that it was not so much the liquor I was trying to side-track as my old schoolfellow.

He walked with me for quite a distance; and he talked more volubly than was his wont. He talked excitedly; and his eyes searched the streets ahead as they widened out before our steps, or as they were instantly and largely visible when we turned a corner. A certain malicious feeling was in my mind as we paced together; I thought:

"There is no public-house on this road."

Before we parted he borrowed a half-sovereign from me, saying that he would pay it back in a day or two, but I cheerfully bade adieu to the coin as I handed it over, and thought also that I was bidding a lengthy adieu to him.

"I won't meet him for quite a while," I said to myself; and that proved to be true.

III

NEVERTHELESS when a fair month had elapsed I did meet him again, and we marched together in a silence which was but sparsely interrupted by speech.

He had apparently prospected my new route, for he informed me that a certain midway side-street was a short cut; and midway in this side-street we found a public-house.

I went into this public-house with the equable pulse of a man who has no true grievance; for I should have been able to provide against a contingency which even the worst equipped prophet might have predicted.

As often as his glass was emptied I saw that it was refilled; but, and perhaps with a certain ostentation, I refrained myself from the cup.

Of course, one drink leads to another and the path between each is conversational. My duty it appeared was to supply the drinks, but I thought it just that he should supply the conversation.

I had myself a fund of silence which might have been uncomfortable to a different companion, and against which he was forced to deploy many verbal battalions.

We had now met quite a number of times. He had exhausted our schooldays as a topic; he knew nothing about politics or literature or city scandal, and talk about weather dies of inanition in less than a minute; and yet— he may have groaned at the necessity—there had to be fashioned a conversational bridge which should unite drink to drink, or drinks must cease.

In such a case a man will talk about himself. It is one's last subject; but it is a subject upon which, given the preliminary push, one may wax eternally eloquent.

He rehearsed to me a serial tale of unmerited calamity, and of hardship by field and flood; of woes against which he had been unable to provide, and against which no man could battle; and of accidents so attuned to the chords of fiction that one knew they had to be true. He had been to rustic-sounding places in England and to Spanish-sounding places in America; and from each of these places an undefined but complete misfortune had uprooted him and chased him as with a stick. So by devious, circuitous, unbelievable routes he had come home again.

One cannot be utterly silent unless one is dead, and then possibly one makes a crackle with one's bones; so I spoke:

"You are glad to be home again," I queried.

He was glad; but he was glad dubiously and with reservations. Misfortune had his address, and here or elsewhere could thump a hand upon his shoulder.

His people were not treating him decently, it appeared. They had been content to see him return from outlandish latitudes, but since then they had not given him a fair show.

Domestic goblins hinted at, not spoken, but which one sensed to be grisly, half detached themselves from between the drinks. He was not staying with his people. They made him an allowance. You could not call it an allowance either: they paid him a weekly sum. Weekly sum was a large way of putting it, for you cannot do much on fifteen shillings a week: that sum per week would hardly pay for, for—

"The drinks," I put in brightly; for one cannot be persistently morose in jovial company.

"I must be off," I said, and I filled the chink of silence which followed on my remark with a waving hand and the bustle of my hasty departure.

IV

Two evenings afterward he met me again.

We did not shake hands; and my salutation was so brief as not really to merit that name.

He fell in beside me and made a number of remarks about the weather; which, if they were as difficult to make as they were to listen to, must have been exceedingly troublesome to him. One saw him searching as in bottomless pits for something to say; and he hauled a verbal wisp from these profundities with the labour of one who drags miseries up a mountain.

The man was pitiable, and I pitied him. I went alternately hot and cold. I blushed for him and for myself; for the stones under our feet and for the light clouds that went scudding above our heads; and in another instant I was pale with rage at his shameful, shameless persistence. I thrust my hands into my pockets, because they were no longer hands but fists; and because they tingled and were inclined to jerk without authority from me.

We came to the midway, cross-street which as well as being a short cut was the avenue to a public-house; and he dragged slightly at the crossing as I held to my course.

"This is the longest way," he murmured.

"I prefer it," I replied.

After a moment he said:

"You always go home this way."

"I shall go a different way to-morrow," I replied.

"What way?" he enquired timidly.

"I must think that out," said I.

With that I stood and resolutely bade him good-bye. We both moved a pace from each other, and then he turned again, flurriedly, and asked me for the loan of half a crown. He wanted it to get a—a—a—

I gave it to him hurriedly and walked away, prickling with a sensation of weariness and excitement as of one who has been worried by a dog but has managed to get away from it.

Then I did not see him for two days, but of course I knew that I should meet him, and the knowledge was as exasperating as any kind of knowledge could be.

V

Ir was quite early in the morning; and he was waiting outside my house. He accompanied me to the tram, and on the way asked me for half a crown. I did not give it, and I did not reply to him.

As I was getting on the tram he lowered his demand and asked me urgently for sixpence. I did not answer nor look at him, but got on my tram and rode away in such a condition of nervous fury that I could have assaulted the conductor who asked me to pay my fare.

When I reached home that evening he was still waiting for me; at least, he was there, and he may have hung about all day; or he may have arrived just in time to catch me.

At the sight of him all the irritation which had almost insensibly been adding to and multiplying and storing itself in my mind, fused together into one sole consciousness of rage which not even a language of curses could make explicit enough to suit my need of expression. I swore when I saw him; and I cursed him openly when he came to me with the sly, timid, outfacing bearing, which had become for me his bearing.

He began at once; for all pretence was gone, and all the barriers of reserve and decency were down. He did not care what I thought of him: nor did he heed in the least what I said to him. He did not care about anything except only by any means; by every means; by cajolery, or savagery, or sentimentality, to get or screw or torment some money out of me.

I knew as we stood glaring and panting that to get the few pence he wanted he would have killed me with as little compunction as one would kill a moth which had fluttered into the room; and I knew that with as little pity I could have slaughtered him as he stood there.

He wanted sixpence, and I swore that I would see him dead before I gave it to him. He wanted twopence and I swore I would see him damned before I gave him a penny.

I moved away, but he followed me clawing my sleeve and whining:

"Twopence: you can spare twopence: what is twopence to you? If I had twopence and a fellow asked me for it I'd give it to him: twopence . . ."

I turned and smashed my fist into his face. His head jerked upwards, and he went staggering backwards and fell backwards into the road; as he staggered the blood jetted out of his nose.

He picked himself up and came over to me bloody, and dusty, and cautious, and deprecating, with a smile that was a leer. . . .

"Now will you give me twopence?" he said.

I turned then and I ran from him as if I were running for my life. As I went I could hear him padding behind me, but he was in no condition, and I left him easily behind. And every time I saw him after that I ran.

ETCHED IN MOONLIGHT

TO

MARY AND CORNELIUS J. SULLIVAN

ETCHED IN MOONLIGHT

I

H<small>E</small> waved his pipe at me angrily:

"Words," he said. "We are doped with words, and we go to sleep on them and snore about them. So with dream. We issue tomes about it, and we might as well issue writs for all the information we give."

I halted him there, for I respect science and love investigation.

"Scientists don't claim to give answers to the riddles of existence," I expostulated, "their business is to gather and classify whatever facts are available, and when a sufficient number of these have been collected there is usually found among them an extra thing which makes examination possible."

"Hum!" said he.

"The difficulty lies in getting all the facts, but when these are given much more is given; for if a question can be fully stated the answer is conveyed in the question."

"That's it," said he, "they don't know enough, but there is a wide pretence——"

"More a prophecy than a pretence. They really state that this or that thing is knowable. It is only that you live hurriedly, and you think everything else should be geared up to your number."

"And they are so geared, or they would not be visible and audible and tangible to me. But a ghost is geared differently to me; and I think that when I am asleep and dreaming I am geared differently to the person who is talking to you here."

"Possibly."

"Certainly. Look at the time it has taken you and me to chatter our mutual nonsense. In an instant of that time I could have had a dream; and, in its infinitesimal duration, all the adventures and excitements of twenty or forty years could take place in ample and leisurely sequence. Someone has measured dream, and has recorded that elaborate and complicated dreams covering years of time can take place while you would be saying knife."

"It was du Prell," I said.

"Whoever it was, I've seen a person awake and talking, but sleepy; noted that person halt for the beat of a word in his sentence, and continue with the statement that he has had a horrible dream. It must have taken place in the blink of an eye. There is no doubt that while we are asleep a power is waking in us which is more amazing than any function we know of in waking life. It is lightning activity, lightning order, lightning intelligence; and that is not to be considered as rhetoric, but as sober statement. The proposition being, that in sleep the mind does actually move at the speed of lightning."

He went on more soberly:

"Last night I had a dream, and in it twenty good years were lived through with all their days and nights in the proper places; and a whole chain of sequential incidents working from the most definite beginning to the most adequate end—and perhaps it all took place between the beginning and the ending of a yawn."

"Well, let us have the dream," said I; for it is clear that you are spoiling to tell it."

He devoted himself anew for a few moments to his pipe and to his thoughts, and, having arranged that both of these were in working order, he recommenced:

"After all this you will naturally expect that something dramatic or astonishing should follow; but it is not surprise, not even interest that is the centre of my thought about this dream. The chief person in the dream was myself; that is certain. The feeling of identity was complete during the dream; but my self in the dream was as unlike my self sitting here as you and I are unlike each other. I had a different physique in the dream; for, while I am now rather dumpish and fair and moonfaced, I was, last night, long and lean as a rake, with a black thatch sprouting over a hatchet head. I was different mentally; my character was not the one I now recognise myself by; and I was capable of being intrigued by events and speculations in which the person sitting before you would not take the slightest interest."

He paused for a few seconds as though reviewing his memories; but, on a movement from me, he continued again, with many pauses, and with much snorings on his pipe, as tho' he were drawing both encouragement and dubiety from it.

"Of course I am romantically minded. We all are; the cat and the dog are. All life, and all that is in it, is romantic, for we and they and it are growing into a future that is all mystery out of a past not less mysterious; and the fear or hope that reaches to us from these extremes are facets of the romance which is life or consciousness, or whatever else we please to name it.

"But," he said, energetically, "I do not pine to rescue a distressed dragon from a savage maiden; nor do I dream of myself dispensing life and death and immortality with a spoon. Life is Romance; I am living and I am Romance; and that adventure is as much as I have the ability to embark on.

"Well, last night, in a dream, I was a person natively capable of such embarkations; and altho' I did not rescue anything from anybody, I am sure I should have done it as one to the manner born. And that character fitted me there, then, as a cat fits into its skin.

"In the dream I was unmistakable I, but

I was not this I, either physically, mentally, or temperamentally.

"And the time was different. I don't know what date it was, but it was not to-day. I don't know what place it was, but it was not this place. I was acting in a convention foreign to the one we act in, and I was acting from an historical or ancestral convention which has no parallel in these times. I don't remember what language I was speaking. I don't remember the names of the people I was in contact with; nor do I recollect addressing anybody by name. I was too familiar with them to require such explanatory symbols. You and I have been chattering these years—do we ever call one another by a name? There is no need to do so; and there was no need to do so with the people of my dream."

He halted, regarding me.

"Do you believe in reincarnation?" he said.

"Do not push casual mountains on my head," I replied, "but get on with the dream."

"Well," said he, "I dreamed a dream and here is the dream."

II

My mind was full of disquietude, impatience, anger; and as the horse stretched and eased under me I dwelt on my own thought. I did not pursue it, for I was not actively thoughtful. I hatched it. I sat on a thought and kept it warm and alive without feeling any desire to make it grow.

"She shall end it to-day," I thought in summary.

And then:

I'll end it to-day.

And thereon I ceased thinking, for when the will has been invoked a true, the truest, act of being has been accomplished, and the mind, which never questions the will, may go on holiday. As against willing all thought is a form of laziness, and my thought, having in that realm neither business nor interest, went lazily to the

nearest simple occurrence that could employ
it, and I became only a person on a horse;
listening to the horse; looking at it; feeling
it with my limbs and feeling myself by its aid.

There was great pleasure in the way my
legs gripped around that warm barrel: in
the way my hands held the beast's head up;
in the way my waist and loins swayed and
curved with the swaying and curving of the
animal. I touched her with my toe and
tapped her neck; and on the moment she
'ossed her head, shaking a cascade of mane
about my hands; gathered her body into a
bunch of muscles, and unloosed them again in
a great gallop; while from behind the hooves
of my servant's beast began to smack and pelt.

In some reaches the surrounding country
flowed into and over the track; and everywhere in its length the grass threw a sprinkle
of green. There were holes here and there;
but more generally there were hollows
which had been holes, and which had in
time accumulated driftage of one kind or
another, so that they had a fullish appearance
without having anything of a level look;
but on the whole I knew of worse roads, and
this one was kept in tolerable repair.

Not far from this place we left the road and struck along a sunken path all grown over at the top with shadowing trees; and so to another and much better-kept road, and on this one I shook out the reins and we went galloping.

It was not unknown to me, this place. Indeed it was so well known that I had no need to look to one side or the other, for everything that was to be seen had been seen by me many hundreds of times; and, if we except grass and trees and grazing cattle, there was nothing to be seen.

Here and there rude dwellings came to view. Low shanties patched together with mud and rock, and all browned and baked by the sun and the rain; and as I rode, these small habitations became more numerous, and from them dogs and children swarmed, snarling and yelping and squeaking.

Again these fell behind, and on another turn a great park came to the view; and across it a building showed gaunt and massive, with turrets at the corners and in front, and the black silhouettes of men were moving in those airy tops.

III

My horse pulled up, all spread-eagled and
snorting, before a flight of stone steps, before
which and on which armed men were clustered
and pacing, and I went up those steps as one
having right of entry. At the top I stood
for an instant to look back on the rolling
grass through which I had galloped a minute
before.

The evening was approaching. Ragged
clouds, yet shot with sunlight, were piling
in the sky, and there was a surmised but
scarcely perceptible greyness in the air.
Over the grass silence was coming, almost
physically, so that the armed rattle and tramp
and the chatter of voices about me had a
detached sound, as though these were but
momentary interruptions of the great silence
that was on its way. That quietude, pre-

monition of silence, brings with it a chill to the heart; as tho' an unseen presence whispered something, unintelligible but understood; conveying a warning that the night comes, that silence comes, that an end comes to all movement of mind and limb.

For when I parted from my horse I parted from my mood; and was again a discontented person, filled with an impatience that seethed within me as water bubbles in a boiling pot.

"She," I thought, "shall choose to-day whether she likes to or not."

And, having expressed itself, my will set in that determination as a rock is set in a stream.

A person came to my beckoning finger, and replied to my enquiry—

"Your honour is expected. Will your honour be pleased to follow me?"

She was sitting in the midst of a company and on my approach gave me her hand to kiss. I saluted it half kneeling, and raking her eyes with a savage stare, which she returned with the quiet constancy to which I was accustomed and which always set me wild, so that the wish I had to beat her was

only laid by the other—and overflowing—
desire I had to kiss her.

I rose to my feet, stepped some paces back,
and the conversation I had interrupted
recommenced.

I was intensely aware of her and of myself;
but saving for us the place was empty for me.
I could feel my chin sinking to my breast;
feel my eyes strained upwards in my bent
face; feel my body projecting itself against
the lips I stared at; and I knew that she was
not unaware of me.

As she spoke, her eyes strayed continually
to me, carelessly, irresistibly, and swung
over or under me and would not look at me.
She could do that while she was talking,
but while she was listening she could only
half do it; for when her tongue was stilled
I caught her mind or her body and held her
and drew her; so that, would she or would
she not, she had to look at me. And I
delighted in that savage impression of
myself upon her; following her nerves with
the cunning of one who could see within her;
and guiding her, holding her, all the time
to me, to me, to me. . . . And then she
looked, and I was baffled anew; for her eye

was as light, as calm, as inexpressive as the bright twinkle of a raindrop that hangs and shivers on a twig.

But the game was broken by a tap on my shoulder, and, at the moment, her voice stumbled on the word she was uttering, her eyes leaped into mine and looked there, and then she was talking again and merry and gracious.

It is a little difficult to explain these things, for I can give no name to the people I am speaking of; nor can I say how I was known to them; but I knew their names and qualities well and they knew mine: so, at the tap on my shoulder, I, knowing whom I should see, turned my eyes to that direction, and saw, for our brows were level, a great golden head, great blue eyes and, just under the rim of vision, a great pair of shoulders.

Everything about him was great in bulk and in quality, and with the exception of our mistress, I had never met one so founded in strength and security as he was.

We turned amicably and went from the room together; out of the great building and across the fields; and as our feet moved rhythmically in the grass we smiled at each other, for indeed I loved him as my own soul and he loved me no less.

As we paced in long slow strides the darkness had already begun to be visible, for the second half of twilight was about us. Away in the direction towards which we trod an ashen sky kept a few dull embers, where, beyond sight, down on the rim of the horizon, the sun had set.

There was silence except for the innumerable rustling bred of grass and quiet trees and a wind too delicate to be heard and scarcely to be felt; for, though the skies were brisk, there was but little ground wind. Naught moved in the trees but the high tender branches that swayed lazily and all alone; leading their aery existence so far from my turbulence of passion that I chid them for their carelessness of one, who, in the very cleft of anxiety, could find an instant to remember them in.

At a time, even while we strode forward, we turned again and retraced our steps; and my mind took one shade more of moodiness. It was he had turned and not I. It was he always who did the thing that I was about to do one moment before I could do it; and he did it unthinkingly, assuredly; with no idea that rebellion might be about him; or that, being there, it could become manifest.

We re-entered and sat to meat with a great company, and she spoke to us equally and frankly and spoke to others with the gracious ease which was never for a moment apart from her.

But I, brooding on her, intent on her as with internal ears and eyes and fingers, felt in her an unwonted excitement, touched something in her which was not usual. When she looked at me that feeling was intensified; for her bright, brief glance, masked as it was and careless as it seemed, held converse with me, as thought in some realm of the spirit we were in unguarded communion.

We were close together then; nearer to each other than we should be again; so close that I could feel with a pang by what a distance we might be separated; and could feel with doubled woe that she grieved for that which she could not comfort.

We left the table.

Little by little the company separated into

small companies, and in a while the great room was boisterous with conversation. They had withdrawn and were talking earnestly together; and I was roving about the room, sitting for a breath with this company and that; listening to my neighbours with an ear that was hearkening elsewhere; and replying to them in terms that might or might not have been relevant to the subject I chanced on.

But in all my movements I managed to be in a position from which I could watch those two; so close in converse, so grave in their conduct of it; so alive to all that was happening about them; and yet sunk spheres below the noise and gaiety of our companions.

Her eye looked into mine, calling to me; and at the signal I left my sentence at its middle and went towards them.

Crossing the room I had a curious perception of their eyes as they watched me advancing; and, for the first time, I observed the gulf which goes about all people and which isolates each irreparably from his fellows. A sense of unreality came upon me, and, as I looked on them, I looked on mystery; and they, staring at me, saw the unknown walking to them on legs. At a stroke we had become strangers, and all the apprehension of strangers looked through our eyes.

She arose when I came within a few paces of them.

"Let us go out," said she.

And we went out quietly.

IV

AGAIN I was in the open. I breathed deeply of the chill air as though drawing on a fount of life; as though striving to draw strength and sustenance and will into my mind.

But the time had come to put an end to what I thought of evasively as "all this"; for I was loath to submit plainly to myself what "all this" noted. I took my will in my hand, as it were, and became the will to do, I scarcely knew what; for to one unused to the discipline and use of will there is but one approach to it, and it is through anger. The first experience of willing is brutal; and it is as though a weapon of offence, a spear or club, were in one's hand; and as I walked I began to tingle and stir with useless rage.

For they were quiet, and against my latent

impetuosity they opposed that massive barrier from which I lapsed back helplessly.

Excitement I understood and loved; the quicker it mounted, the higher it surged, the higher went I. Always above it, master of it. Almost I was excitement incarnate; ready for anything that might befall, if only it were heady and masterless. But the quietude of those left me like one in a void, where no wing could find a grip and where I scarce knew how to breathe.

It was now early night.

The day was finished and all that remembered the sun had gone. The wind which had stirred faintly in tall branches had lapsed to rest. No breath moved in the world, and the clouds that had hurried before were quiet now, or were journeying in other regions of the air. Clouds there were in plenty; huge, pilings of light and shade; for a great moon, burnished and thin, and so translucent that a narrowing of the eyes might almost let one peer through it, was standing far to the left; and in the spaces between the clouds there was a sharp scarce glitter of stars.

There was more than light enough to walk by; for that great disc of the heavens poured a radiance about us that was almost as bright as day.

Now as I walked the rage that had begun to stir within ceased again, and there crept into me so dull a lassitude that had death stalked to us in the field I should not have stepped from his way.

I surrendered everything on the moment; and, for the mind must justify conduct, I justified myself in the thought that nothing was worth this trouble; and that nothing was so desirable but it could be matched elsewhere, or done without.

It is true that the mind thinks only what desire dictates; and that when desire flags thought will become ignoble. My will had flagged, for I had held it too many hours as in a vice; and I was fatigued with that most terrible of exercises.

The silence of those indomitable people weighed upon me; and the silence of the night, and the chill of that large, white moon burdened me also. Therefore, when they came to talk to me, I listened peacefully; if one may term that state of surrender peace. I listened in a cowardly quietness; replying more by a movement of the hands than by words; and when words were indispensable making brief use of them.

It was she who spoke, and her tone was gentle and anxious and official:

"We have arranged to marry," said she.

To that I made no reply.

I took the information on the surface of my mind as one receives an arrow on a shield, and I did not permit it to enter further. There, in neutral ground, the sentence lay; and there I could look on it with the aloof curiosity of one who examines an alien thing.

"They were going to get married!" Well . . . But what had it to do with me? Everyone got married sometime, and they were going to get married. This was a matter in which I had no part, for they were not going to get married to me: they were going to marry each other; it was all no business of mine.

So a weary brain thinks weary thoughts; and so I thought; separating myself languidly from the business of those who were making me a partner in their affairs. All I desired was that the explanations should cease, and that I might heave myself into a saddle and jog quietly to my own place.

But I knew, almost with sickness, that I could not go until this sentence had been explained and re-explained. They would inevitably consider that I could not grasp its swollen import until they had spoken under it and over it; and explained that there was a necessity for it; and detailed me that also.

I could foresee a dreary hour that would drone and drone with an unending amplification of duty and interest and love, and a whole metaphysic to bind these together.

Love! They would come to that at last. But when they dared the word they would not leave it while they had a tooth to put into it.

They would tell me around it and about; and the telling would excite them to a fury of retelling. I should have its history, and all the din and crackle of all the words that could be remembered on that subject or germain to it.

I found it happen so.

I was initiated into the secrets of their duty to their people and to themselves. I learned the intricacy of the interests wherein all parties were involved; until it was impossible to tell where duty ended and interest began. And, in the inevitable sequel, I was the confidant of their love. And I listened to that endless tale with the drowsy acquiescence of one moonstruck and gaping . . . drowsily nodding; murmuring my yes and yes drowsily. . . .

They were good to me. They were sisterly and brotherly to me. By no hairsbreadth of reticence was I excluded from their thoughts, their expectations, their present felicity, and their hopes of joy to come. For two people going alone may have verbal and bodily restraint but the company of a third will set them rabid. It is as though that unnecessary presence were a challenge, or a query, which they must dispose of or die. Therefore, and because of me, they had to take each other's hand. They had to fondle paw within paw; and gaze searchingly on each other and on me; with, for me, a beam of trust and brotherliness and inclusion which my mood found sottish.

They were in love.

They whispered it to each other. They said it loudly to me. And more loudly yet they urged it, as though they would proclaim it to the moon. . . . And about their hands was a vile activity; a lust of catching; a fever of relinquishing; for they could neither hold nor withhold their hands from each other.

"Do they expect me to clasp their hands together, and hold them so that they shall not unloose again? Do they wish me to draw their heads together, so that they may kiss by compulsion? Am I to be the page of love and pull these arms about each other?"

We walked on, heedless of time; and I heedless of all but those voices that came to me with an unending, unheard, explanation; the voices of those who cared naught for me; who cared only that I was there, an edge to their voluptuousness.

V

BUT when one walks one arrives somewhere. If the environment had not changed we might have gone on for ever. This walk and talk had grown into us like a monstrous habit from which we could not break away; and until a change came to the eye our minds could not swerve from the world they were building nor our feet from the grasses we walked on.

A change did occur, mercifully; the little variety which might deturn that level of moonbred, lovesick continuity or inertia; for we think largely through the eyes, or our thoughts flow easily to the direction in which our gaze is set.

The great park, waving with separated trees, came abruptly to an end.

At this step it was yet a sward. But ten

paces beyond it was a rubble of bush and rock, unkempt as a beggarman's beard. Everywhere there were bits of walls with crumbling ledges up which the earth was gradually mounting and which the grass had already conquered.

Under the beam of that great flat moon the place seemed wildly beautiful; with every mound a glory of silver and peace, and every hollow a pit of blackness and mystery. A little beyond, perfect, although in the hub and centre of ruin, a vast edifice reared against the sky, and it shone white as snow in the moonlight except where a projecting battlement threw an ebon shade.

"The old castle," said she, "I have not walked this way in ten years."

And, saying so, she walked to it.

I had never been that way, and I looked on that massive pile of silence almost with expectation, as tho' a door might open and something emerge, or a voice roar rustily at us from the moon-clad top.

It was old, and it was built as they built of old and build no more; for the walls were fifteen feet thick, and time might have sat before it through half-eternity marvelling by what arts such a solidity could possibly be reduced.

We paced about it, wondering at it, and at the silence which came to and from it; and marvelling that men had with such patience consummated so vast a labour; for the lives of generations had passed e'er this was ended and secure.

There was but one door, and we came on this in our silent walk. It was swung to, but was yet open just a little; barely a foot of opening; a dense black slit in the moonlight.

"I must slip in," said she.

He smiled at her, catching again her hand. And into his ear, but with her eyes fixed on mine, she said:

"I want to whisper something in the ear of silence and desolation."

She slipped within; and, when in, she pulled at his hand. With a look at me half laughing, half apologetic, he squeezed after her; and I was alone staring at the bossed and plated door.

There was silence without and within, but

I found that my eyes were fixed on that silence within; and from it, as I expected, almost as I willed, there came, as though bred from the silence, a sound. It was ten times more discreet than a whisper, and was to be heard only by an ear that knew it would come.

A sudden panic leaped within my heart and rolled into my ears like a beaten drum; and that rage of fear was my memory, sprung suddenly from nowhere, of the hands that had gripped and released each other; of the eyes that had flashed upon eye and lip; of the bodies that had swung tenderly sideways and fell languidly away again.

And at that my mind emptied itself of thought, and I saw nothing, heard nothing, was nothing. Only in my head there came again a sudden great throb as though a muffled bell had thudded inside it. My hands went out without any direction from me; they gripped on the door; and, with the strength of ten men, I pulled on it.

It fell to with a crash which might have been heard about the earth; and yet which let through one infinitesimal fraction of sound; a beginning of sound only; so tiny, it could scarcely be heard, so tense that the uproar of doom could not have covered that sound from my ear.

It began and it never finished, for it never continued. Its beginning was caught and prevented; but within my ear it continued and completed itself, as a scream which I should never cease to hear; while still with hanging jaw and fixed eyes I stared at the closed door.

I walked away.

I turned from the place and went slowly in the direction we had come.

I was a walking statue; a bodily movement only; for the man within had temporarily ceased to be. Within I was a silence brooding on silence and darkness. No smallest thought, no stir towards thinking crept in my mind; but yet I was not quite as a dead man walking, for something was happening . . . I was listening. I was listening for them to speak in my heart. . . .

And then I began to run; a steady pelt of running, as though I could run away from them, mewed in that stony den, and yet liable to shriek on me from the centre of my being.

Again the change to the eye brought change to the mind; and when I sighted the great building all glimmering with lights I came to my breathless self.

I went to the stables; found my man; and in five minutes was in the saddle, and, with him behind, went plunging through the darkness towards my own place.

How often during that ride did I clench my hand to pull on the rein and go back to release them. Every minute, every second, I was going to do it. But every minute, every second, my hand refrained from pulling on the horse, and my heels gave her notice to go yet faster.

For I was not quite a man. I was an inertia . . . or I was the horse. I was something that ran; and my whole being was an unexpressed wish to run and never stop. I did not even wish to come to my place; for, arriving there, I must halt and dismount, and fumble and totter among obstacles of doors and people. . . .

That halt had to come; and I dismounted in a mood that merged rapidly from impatience to anger, and from that to almost blind fury. In a little while my dispositions were made, and I was on the road again on a fresh beast, a bag of money and valuables strapped on the nag, and behind me two servants coming on at a gallop.

I was running away from the country. I was running away from those two mewed in the prison to which nobody knew they had gone. But more urgently even than that I was running away from myself.

VI

THERE comes an interval which my recollection would figure as ten or twelve years.
During this time I did not return to my own
country, and, so far as was possible, I did
not even think of it.

For it was in my nature to forget easily;
or, by an effort of the will, to prevent
myself remembering whatever I considered
inconvenient or distressing. I could put
trouble to one side as with a gesture, and
this trouble I put away and did not again
admit into mind.

But a trouble that is buried is not disposed
of. Be the will ever so willing, the mind
ever so obedient, a memory cannot be
destroyed until it has reached its due time
and evolved in its proper phases.

A memory may die in the mind as peacefully as an old man dies in his bed; and it will rest there tranquilly, and moulder into true forgetfulness, as the other débris moulders into dust. But a memory cannot be buried alive; for in this state of arrested being, where it can neither grow old nor die, it takes on a perpetual unused youth, and lies at the base of one's nature as an unheard protest; calling to the nerves instead of to the brain, and strumming on these with an obstinate patience and an unending fertility of resource.

It has been banished from the surface to the depths; and in the deep of being, just beyond the borders of thought, it lies, ready as at the lifting of a finger to leap across these borders, as new and more poignant than at its creation.

Upon those having the gift of mental dismissal a revenge is taken. They grow inevitably irritable; and are subject to gusts of rage so unrelated to a present event that their contemporaries must look upon them as irresponsible.

A buried thought like a buried body will rot; and it will spread a pestilence through the moral being that is its grave or its gaoler.

It was so with me.

From being one frank and impetuous and careless, I became moody, choleric, suspicious; and so temperamentally unstable that as I could not depend on myself so no one else could depend on me either.

All things that were commenced by me had to be finished by another; for in the very gust and flooding of success I would throw myself aside from it; or bear myself so outrageously that my companions would prefer failure and my absence to a success which had me within a league of the prize.

Everything, even a memory, must be faced at last. No man can rest until he has conquered or surrendered to his enemy; for, be success attained or failure, a legitimate bourne is reached wherein the mind may acquiesce and be at one with the result.

So, one day, I unburied my dead; looking upon it with a curiosity and fear which were the equal of each other; and having once looked I could not forbear to look again; until I became a patient, timid devotee of my own evil.

A treacherous story in truth; and if repentance could have retrieved my crime how quickly it had been erased. But the fact of repentance comes home only to the person in fault. It has no value for the victim; for a man may outrun the laws of man, but the law of his self he can neither distance nor dodge.

Half the value of an act is its reaction, for the one pays and completes the other. My act was vanity and here came shame to make of it a total; and there, in the mixture of the two, was I, fully expressed and condemned. Vanity had sentenced me to shame; and shame would take up the tale again with vanity, and would lead me to the further justice of which I had need. For that which we do outwardly we do inwardly. We condemn or reward ourselves in every action; and the punishment we receive is due to us in a sense deeper than that indicated in the word retribution.

I thought of those two; and I thought of them shyly as one who no longer had the right even to remember them. For they had counted on my nature, as they judged it; on my honour as they knew it; and on my friendship as they thought to have proved it. But into these aspects of me they had been sucked as into a bog. I had given way under their feet and they had sunk into and died in me.

Was it a wonder that I fled across the fields fearful lest they might scream to me from my soul? Alas, it was there they had been betrayed, and there were buried; wherever else their bones might whiten.

And now I began to brood on them deeply and perpetually, until nothing in the world was so important as they were, and they became me almost in my entirety.

I reconstructed them and myself, and the happy days which had preceded that most wicked of hours; and I knew that, whatever other enmity or suspicion had been in the world, there had been naught but friendship between us and the frankest and freest trust. I had reason to trust them, and had given them occasion to believe that in my keeping their honour and their all was safe; and to that trust I had given the lie at the moment of its reposal.

Indeed I was stupefied to think that I had committed this baseness; for on behalf of these two I would have counted on my own loyalty with as little calculation as they had.

There was indeed something to be said for me if that enquiry were rigorously pursued. But it was a poor thing and only to be advanced in my favour for it could not be urged.

She had halted between us for a long time; not balancing our values or possibilities; but humanly unwilling to judge, and womanly unable to wound. That delicate adjustment could not have continued indefinitely; but it would have continued longer had I not forced the issue, or stated the position; and once that a case is truly stated nothing remains but the judgment which is already apparent in the statement.

It was I had failed in the trial. I whose nerves gave way. I who became impatient and would gamble on the chance; and the gambler is always an incomplete man. In all real things the gambler must lose, for he is staking on chance that which can only be won by the knowledge which is concreted merit; and in all memorable deeds the personality must win, and chance have not even the ghost of a chance.

They had bettered me; and, although they were dead and I alive, they were beyond me and topped me as a lion tops a dog.

So, pride having proved to me that I was treacherous, shame came to teach me the great lesson of life; for in humility the mind is released from fleshy fogs and vapours; and in that state only can it be directed to its single natural work, the elucidation of character.

Ideas which enter the mind only have no motive force—they are alive, but have not yet energy. They exist but as subjects of conversation, as intellectual gossip, but before a thought can become an act it must sink deeper than the mind and into the imagination where abides the true energy of all thinking creatures. It is not the mind but the imagination that sets the will to work; and both mind and will obey it instantly, as a horse winces instantly to the touch of a spur.

So these two, having got into my imagination, could not be let out again, until it was satisfied that all which could be done was done, and a moral as well as a logical end arrived at.

I took to horse, therefore, and set out for home.

VII

APART from my adventure with those people my memory is blurred. My dealings and encounters with them are distinct as though they happened to-day; but the portions of the narrative interspacing that adventure have already more than half faded from memory. Yet it seems to me that my journey back was a long one, and that ships had to be taken as well as horses ere I had returned and could recognise landmarks and faces.

In many of these recognitions the passage of time was marked for me as tho' it had been written.

Here was a dwelling which had not before been here: and in this place, where a house had been, there was a roofless ruin.

Here a man tended his sheep. When I

passed the last time he had not been old; but his beard had whitened as though in one night of snow.

I passed youths and girls who knew me and stood aside; but they had changed from the children I might have remembered into lusty and lengthy and unknown people.

The word that I was coming must have far preceded me, for these people recognised me with curiosity but without astonishment; and in my own house I was clearly expected and welcomed with all the preparedness a master might hope for.

I had not hoped for any welcome, and would have preferred to come back as anonymously as a bird does who returns to its last year's hedge; for, although I did not wish to escape anything that might be in keeping for me, I did desire to inform myself of the circumstances by which I should be surrounded, and the dangers that I might have to front.

There was no hint of danger or disquietude among my people. Their welcome was as free, their service as easy and accustomed as though I had returned from a visit to the next town. And the marvel of this almost stupefied me; while the impossibility of demanding direct information from those unsupicious people plunged me in dismay.

I thought to myself—"The bodies have never been found, and, by some extraordinary chance, suspicion has not turned upon me for their disappearance."

At the thought a weight was lifted from my soul; but only for a moment; for I had not come back in search of security, but in order that whatever debt was due by me should be paid.

But I had to know how things were, and, after eating, the man of whom I enquired, replied that my return was known at the Castle (as I shall call it) and that a visit from its chatelains was expected on the next day to welcome me home.

With this news my alarm vanished and an almost excessive joy took its place. My mind lightened, and poured into my body, as from a fountain, well-being and energy.

For how long? Was it more than ten minutes? ten seconds? The mind that can hold joy must be strong indeed. I could no more contain it than I could round the sea in my palm; and, almost as it had swirled into me, it swept out; leaving behind only that to which I had a right and which was my own.

Nothing happens without mental acquiescence, and that which had emptied my mind of joy and my body of buoyancy was the memory that I should see them on the morrow, and, with that memory, egotism pushed up its head and I thought—"They will not meet the unfledged youngster they parted from!"

That was all. But it was sufficient to ride me as I would ride a horse, and to pull me round to its direction, and to the vanity I imagined to have left behind.

I chid myself for a fool. I looked back with a lightning eye on the wasted years; the useless misery; the unnecessary toil and sordid excitement through which I had passed; and at a stroke my mind became filled with a tumult and admixture of emotions which no one word would synthesise, nor could I describe them in many words.

In undisciplined minds a conflict of thought will provoke anger or sleep; but in almost any mind a conflict of emotion will breed rage; and, for the mind is lazy, a thought will seek for an emotion to rest on, and will lie in it as in a bed. So nobility rots in dream, and action grows stagnant in imagining itself. Behind life is laziness, and from it, in direct descent or ascent, is desire and lust and anger, which master words describe up to a point the world and its working.

Thus, having torn mself out of anger as from a pit, I hurried back to it, and I found that I was thinking of my coming visitors with a dislike which was as near to hatred as I could arrive at.

They were alive, and I had paid for their death! I had wasted myself and my years grieving for them; repenting for them; idealising them in a dull torment and agitation of nerve and brain!

For nothing! And nothing became symbolised by them. They stood for it: they were Nothing; and, with that, vanity was in possession again, for I stood for something as against their nothing; and all the coil of pride and shame and payment had to recommence.

VIII

THEY came, and for a time resentment was covered by curiosity; and while we talked together I found myself glancing at one and the other with the curiosity of him who peeps at a camel or a criminal.

There was a difference in them, but it was not essential; it was only the change which comes with the passage of time.

All that I remembered was here, but more pronounced. What had been quietude had deepened to tranquillity. All that sense of certainty and command was more certain and commanding, for ease and power and good humour was as unconsidered and native a part of them as their limbs.

He had been great in bulk, he was now huge. He had filled out, and filled in, and he strode and towered like a mountain.

Her I remembered as one remembers a day of April beauty and promise, various with that uncertainty which troubles and delights. Now summer was on her with all its gorgeous endowment.

She was a rest to the eye. She was a benediction to the senses. She calmed desire. For to look on her was to desire no more, and yet to be satisfied. Her beauty was so human, her humanity so beautiful, that she could embrace the thought that would embrace her; and return it absolved, purified, virgin again to the lust that sent it out.

There are beings in this world who are secured against every machination of evil. They live as by divine right, as under divine protection; and when malice looks in their faces it is abashed and must retreat without harming them. All the actions of these are harmonious and harmless and assured; and in no circumstances can they be put in the wrong, nor turned from their purpose. Their trust is boundless, and, as they cannot be harmed, so it cannot be betrayed. They are given their heaven on

earth as others are here given their hell; and
what they get they must have deserved; and
they must indeed be close to divinity.

Of such were these, and I hated them with
a powerlessness which was a rage of humility;
and I mourned for myself as the hare may
mourn who is caught in a trap and knows
that it will kill him.

I did not hate them, for they could not
be hated. My egotism envied them. My
shame, and, from it, my resentment, was
too recent to be laid, though the eyes of a
dove looked into mine and the friendliest
hand was on my shoulder. Something
obstinate within my soul, something over
which I had no charge, stiffened against
them; and if one part of my nature yearned
for surrender and peace the other part held
it back, and so easily that there was never a
question as to where obedience must go.

I was easy with them and as careless as
I had ever been; and the fact that I had not
harmed them put out of my mind the truth
that I had tried to do so. Not by a look, an
intonation, did they show a memory of that
years'-old episode; and what they could
forget I could forget as quickly; or could

replace by the recollection that in a distant time they had set me adrift in a world of torment.

This did not express itself even in my mind. It lay there like a bulk of unthought thought; which, as it was expressed in its entirety and not in its parts, had to be understood by the nerves where the intelligence lacked width and grasp; and there was I again in the trough of the sea and twisting to any wind.

In a little time I had reaccustomed myself to the new order of things. The immediate past of wandering and strife grew less to be remembered, and my new way of life became sequential and expected.

I knew, and there is contentment in that kind of knowledge, exactly what I should do on the morrow; and I might have ventured a prediction as to how I should be employed in the month to come. For life gathered about me in a web of unhasty occupation and untiring leisure; so that the thing to be done and the doing of it flowed sweetly to each other; and all was accomplished without force, and almost without volition.

Many times my horse took that well-remembered road, and it became as natural to me to turn in that direction as to turn to the rooms of my own house. For I found there much that I desired, even unconsciously: friendship, companionship, and, more than all, gaiety; for their young lusty brood began to knit themselves about my life and knot themselves into it.

To go from a sedate, unruffled house into a home that seethes with energy and innocence, and all the animation of budding life, is a notable thing for one who has come to the middle term; and though he had before suffered children with a benevolent impatience he grows to be thankful if they will notice him with even an approach to interest.

It is a blessed thing that whoever wishes to be welcomed benevolently by a child will be so welcomed; for the order of young years is to respond, and they do that without reservation. Children and animals, however we can hurt, we cannot hate; for they are without reserve; and that lack is the one entirely lovable quality in the world.

In the meantime events moved with me, for they, having settled their own lives, charged themselves with the arrangement of mine; and, by a delicate, untiring management, I found myself growing more friendly or more accustomed to a lady of her kin; whom at last, they expected me to marry; who certainly expected to marry me; and whom I should wed when the time came with neither reluctance nor impatience. But this lady I do not remember even slightly. She is a shade; a fading smile, and exists for me as a dream within the dream.

It was settled, and whether I or they or she arranged it I no longer know. It may have been just propinquity, or that sense of endlessness, that inertia of speech, which causes one to continue talking when there is no more to be said; so that, and inevitably, one asks a girl to marry one, there being nothing left to be said; and she, terrified lest silence should fall upon her, agrees to do so, and marvels thereat until she is endlessly wed.

So I asked and she replied; and those who take charge of such arrangements took charge of this; and settled all about time and place, and removed every impediment to our union.

IX

I⊤ was the night before my wedding, and I was filled with that desolation of the traveller who must set forth on the morrow, and does not quite know where he is going, nor why he should go there. I had, as was now my custom, taken horse and gone to the castle. The girl I should marry was there, and those two who walked like gods on the earth and who stirred like worms in my mind.

We talked and ate, but beyond that I can only remember the atmosphere of smiles and kindliness to which I was accustomed.

My recollection begins towards nightfall. I had kissed that girl's hands and she went away to her bed; and I was preparing to perform the same duty to my hostess, when she postponed it.

"It is a lovely night," she said, "and,"

looking at her husband, meaningly, as I thought, "after to-morrow we three shall not be the companions we have been. We shall not meet so often nor so carelessly."

To my glance of enquiry she continued, smilingly:

"A husband belongs to his wife. Your leisure will henceforth have so many claims on it that we may see little of you. When we see you again we may, like drunken men, see you double."

My glance was humorous but questioning.

"Let us take a last walk," she suggested.

"Yes," her husband assented. "One more walk of comrades; one more comfortable talk, and then let to-morrow work what changes it may."

It was a lovely night, with a sky swept bare of all but the moon.

High in the air, bare and bright and round, she rode in beauty.

And, but for her, we might have seen how lonely was the blue serene that swung about her.

Naught stayed in that immense for eye or ear. Naught stirred or crept. All slept but sheer, clear space and silence. And they, with the wonder of the wide, high heaven, were wonderful.

Afar, apart, in lovely alternating jet and silver, the sparse trees dreamed. They seemed as turned upon themselves. As elves they brooded; green in green; whisht and inhuman and serene.

All moved within.

All was indrawn.

All was infolded and in solitude.

The sky, the grass, the very earth rejected knowing; and we hied with the moon as though she and we were atune to naught beside.

Against that blank withdrawal we struggled as the uneasy dead may, who would regain a realm in which they can find no footing. Silence came on us as at a command; and we were separated and segregated, each from the other, and from all things, as by a gulf.

I looked to the faces on either side of me. They were thin and bright and utterly unknown to me. They seemed wild and questing; stern-poised eagle profiles that were alien in every way to the friendly faces I had known.

And I! I could not see my own face, but I could feel it as a blanch of apprehension.

Why should fear thus flood my being? For there was nothing within me but fear. I was a blank that swirled with terror; and was stilled as suddenly to a calmness scarcely less terrifying. I strove to engage my thoughts in common things, and, with that purpose, I scanned on every side so that my mind might follow my eye and be interested in its chances.

But in the moonlight there is no variety. Variety is colour, and there was about me but an universal shimmer and blanch, wherein all shape was suppressed, and nothing was but an endless monotony and reduplication of formless form.

So we went; and in the quietude we paced through and the quietness we brought with us we scarce seemed living beings.

We were spectres going in a spectral world. Although we walked we did not seem to move; for to that petrified universe our movement brought no change; and each step was but an eddy in changeless space.

I looked at them; at those faces cut by the moon to a sternness of stone; and I knew in a flash that I was not going between friends but between guards; and that their intention towards me was pitiless.

My will was free. I could have turned and walked backwards, and they would not have hindered me in any way. But they might have smiled as they turned, and that smile would be deadly as an arrow in the heart.

To dare be a coward how courageous one must be! I thought with envy of those whose resolution is so firm that they can fly from danger while there is yet a chance. But to be a coward and to be afraid to save oneself! Into what a degradation must one have fallen for that!

I clenched my hands, and at the contact of my nails I went cold to the bone.

X

AT a certain moment each of those silver-pale faces seemed to look forward more straitly, more distantly; and I, withdrawing my eyes from the grey-toned vegetation at my feet, looked forward also.

We had reached the extreme of the park. Beyond was a rugged, moon-dozed tumble of earth and bush and rock; and beyond again was the vast silver-shining keep, to which, in years long gone, we three had walked; and from which, and in what agony, I once had fled.

In the miracle we call memory I recovered that night, and was afflicted again with the recollection of clasping and unclasping hands, of swaying bodies, and of meeting and flying eyes.

But the same hands made now no mutual

movement. Those eyes regarded nothing but distance; and those bodies but walked and did no more. It was my hands that twitched and let go; my eyes that stared and flinched away; my body that went forward while its intuition and intention was to go back.

In truth I did halt for a heart's beat; and when I moved again, I was a pace in advance, for they had stayed on the instant and could not move again so quickly as my mood drove.

I looked at them no more. I looked at nothing. My eyes, although wide, were blind to all outward things, and what they were seeking within me it would be hard to tell.

Was I thinking, or feeling or seeing internally? For I was not unoccupied. Somewhere, in unknown regions of my being, there were busynesses and hurryings and a whole category of happenings, as out of my control as were the moods of those who went with me.

All thought is a seeing. No idea is real if it be not visualised. To see is to know; to know is to see clearly, and other knowledge than that is mechanical. But as we cannot see beyond a stated range of vision so we cannot speak beyond a definite range of thought. Fear has never uttered itself; nor has joy; nor any emotion that has quickened beyond normality. These stir in a mood too remote for expression by words that are fashioned to tell the common experiences of sense and its action.

How should I tell that which was happening to me as I trod forward; my face as impassive as theirs, my brow as calm? The reaction to extreme events is in the spine or the pit of the stomach, but the action is elsewhere, and is in an organ uncharted yet by man.

I trod with them, free to all appearance as a man can be, and yet bound by fetters which had been forged through long years by myself for myself.

We halted, and I looked again on the bossed and monumental door which stood in my memory almost as a living thing. It was as it had been formerly. A black gape, little more than a foot wide, yawned from the top to the bottom. I noticed the rough herbage sprouting grossly among pebbles at its foot, and the overhanging jut of harsh stone that crowned or frowned from its top. And then I looked at them.

His gaze was bent on me, massive as the stone itself.

"Go in," he said.

I looked at her, and although her lips said nothing her eyes, gleaming whitely in the moonlight, commanded as sternly as her husband's voice.

"Go in," he said harshly, "as we went in, and get out, if you can, as we got out."

He reached a monstrous hand to my shoulder; but, at my motion to put it aside, he let it fall; and instead his hand took hold of the great knob. I cast one look at the vast, white moon; at the steady blue spaces about it; at the tumbled sparkle that was the world; and, without a word, I squeezed through the narrow aperture.

I turned and looked back. I had one glimpse of a black form set in a dull radiance. Then the door closed on me with a clang that echoed and echoed and echoed in my ears long after its cause had ceased.

XI

It was dark where I was.

It was a darkness such as I had never experienced. The blackness about me was solid as ebony. It was impenetrable to thought itself.

It flooded my brain so that the blindness within me was as desperate as that without. I could not keep my eyes open; for, being open, they saw the darkness. I dared not close them; for, being closed, I became that darkness myself. . . .

And at every moment, from the right hand and the left, from before me and from behind me, I imagined things. Darknesses that could move, silences that could touch. . . .

I dared not realise my speculations, and yet, in lightning hints, my mind leaped at

and fled from thoughts that were inexpress-
ible except as shivers. My flesh twitched
and crept, and I shrank from nothing, as
though it could extend a claw; as though
it could clutch me with an iron fist. . . .

I was standing yet, long after they had
gone, beside the door; fearing to move from
it; afraid to stir; and looking about me, as
it were, with my ears.

I had no anger against them. I was too
occupied for any emotion but those, or that,
which was present. I ceased even to think
about them; or such seconds of thought as
chanced through my agony were humble.
They were not forgiving or regretful; they
were merely humble, as the thoughts of
an overdriven sheep might be towards its
driver.

They were gone; and with them everything had gone. I was surrounded by
nothingness. I was drowned in it. I was
lost and solitary as some grey rock far out in
sea. Nay, for the sun shines on it, the wind
blows, and a gannet halts there and flaps his
wing. There was loneliness nowhere but

where I was. There was not such a silence
even in the tomb as the silence in which I
was centred; for, while the terror of darkness
did not diminish, the horror of silence began
to grow. And it grew as some monstrous
thing may that reproduces itself on itself,
tirelessly, timelessly, endlessly.

Nature abhors a vacuum, and so does the
mind, for the mind is nature. It will contrive
sound when silence oppresses it, and will
people any desolation with its own creatures.
Alas for man! With what pain he can create
how meagre a joy! With what readiness he
can make real a misery!

And my ears had two duties to perform!
They must look for me as well as listen, and
when the mind is occupied in two endeavours
something of craziness comes, even in trivial
things.

I began to hear, and at no time could I
tell what I heard. I began to see, and no
words will impart what I saw. I closed both
eyes and ears with my fingers, and was aware
in a while that my under-jaw was hanging;
that my mouth was open; and that I was
listening and looking through that.

At the knowledge my will awakened, and I placed calmness forcibly on myself as tho' I were casing my soul in mail. I strode firmly to my right hand, and after a few steps I came against a wall. I strode in the opposite direction, and in double the paces I came against a wall. I walked backwards, and in twenty steps I came against a wall; and following this my groping fingers tapped suddenly in space.

There was an aperture. . . .

My hair rose on my head stiff and prickling. I did not dare to enter that void in the void. I should more willingly have leaped into a furnace. I went from it on tip-toe, striving to make no sound lest that hole should hear me, and tread behind. . . .

It would come noiselessly. And yet it would be heard! It would roll gently, overwhelmingly, like some new and unimaginable thunder—

"No . . .!" I said in panic to my soul, as I trod cautiously from that behind.

"Great God!" I thought, as I stood somewhere, for now I had lost all direction, and was nowhere. "Great God, what shall I do?"

I lowered myself secretly to the ground, groping with a blind hand to make sure that nothing was there.

"I will try to sleep," I said in my mind.

Nay, I said it to my mind; striving to command that which I had never learned to control. I huddled my knees up and curved my chin forward like a sleeping dog. I covered my face with my hands, and was still as the stone on which I lay.

"I will try to sleep," I said. "I will think of God," I said.

And it seemed to me that God was the blankness behind, which might advance. And that nothing was so awful as the thought of Him—unimaginable and real! withheld, and imminent, and threatening, and terrific! My knees were listening for Him to the front of me: my back was hearkening from behind; and my brain was engaged elsewhere in matters which I could not cognise.

"If I were to speak aloud!" I thought.

And some part of my mind dared me to do so; wheedled at me to utter one clapping shout: but I knew that at the sound of a voice, of even my own voice, I should die as at a stroke.

XII

How long did that last? Was it an hour, a
year, a lifetime?

Time ceases when emotion begins, and
its mechanical spacings are then of no more
account. Where is time when we sleep?
Where is it when we are angry? There is
no time, there is but consciousness and its
experiences.

I stayed where I had lain myself, and
whether my eyes were open or closed I no
longer knew. The miseries of this place
had abated. No, that does not express it,
for this was no longer a place. This place
had disappeared, or it had been merged in
the new dimension which I call Nowhere.

It is immeasurably great; it is unimagin-
ably small: for as there is no time so there
is no space: there is only being, and its

modes: and in that region my misery continued itself far from the knowledge of this brain and beyond the let or hindrance of this body.

And yet somewhere, somehow, I knew something that I can only think of as nothing. An awful, a deadly business was proceeding, with me as the subject. It can only be expressed negatively. Thus I may phrase it, I had gone in the spirit into that aperture from whch I had fled. I was in contact with the unmanifest, and that, in its own sphere, is as competent and enduring as are its extensions with which we are familiar. But of that I cannot speak; for as it was out of range of these senses so it was out of range of this mind whose sole preoccupation is these senses.

I had been in terror, but in what was I now? IIow little to me was the human absence of light, the normal absence of sound that had frightened me.

I was nowhere, and it was real. I was nothing and I was enduring. I would have returned to my blank, dumb prison as one flies to a paradise, but I could not, for something had happened to me. I was translated; and until that experience was fulfilled I could not regain myself nor evade in any way my happenings.

Therefore, I do not know how long I remained crouched in that stony den. Nor how I lay; nor aught that happened to me. But at a point I did return to normal consciousness, and that as swiftly as though one had taken me by the shoulders and clicked me to another direction.

All that monstrous Something-Nothing ceased; and I was listening with these ears, and staring through known darkness with these eyes that see you.

There were footsteps outside the door, and in an instant the door grinced and screeched and swung.

XIII

IT was those two. But I did not move from where I lay, and when I did so it was because he lifted me. Those giant arms could lift me as one plucks up a cat; and in a moment I was walking, and the arm that was yet around my waist was pressing me lovingly to his side.

"We were only playing with you," he said.

And she at my other side cooed, as she fondled my hand.

"It was only a game."

I looked wordlessly from one to the other and laughed gently.

It was strange that I did not wish to speak. It was strange still that I would not speak; and to everything that they said I returned my gentle laugh. That, it seemed to me,

must be sufficient communion even for them;
and who in the world could wish to speak
when he might laugh?

We walked on, slowly at first, and then
hastily, and sentences came from one to the
other across me; sometimes explanations,
at times assertions and assents.

"It took us ten minutes to get out," he
said, "and we thought——"

"For you are so much cleverer than we
are," she interposed.

"That you would have been home almost
as quickly as we were."

"It took us ten long minutes to imagine
that although the door was closed it might
not be fastened," he went on, "but when I
pulled on it it opened at once.

"I was glad to see the moonlight," he
continued in a tone of reverie.

"Glad!" she exclaimed.

"Those ten minutes were unpleasant," he
assented.

"They were wicked," she exclaimed
energetically. "They——" she paused and
took my arm again: "They are forgotten
and forgiven. Our thoughts of each other
now can be all frankness and trust."

I must have been imprisoned for some hours, for when I went in there had been a bright moon in a bare sky, where now there was no moon and the heavens were deeply shadowed. Our faces were visible to each other as dull shapes, and the spaces about us were bathed in that diaphanous darkness through which one looks without seeing, and against which things loom rather than show.

A wonderful feeling of well-being flowed through me, warming and bracing me. A feeling of astonishing rest for myself, and of endless affection for my companions.

And with it all there was a sense, confused and yet strong, that I knew something which they did not know. That I had a secret which would astonish them when they discovered it.

I knew they should discover it, for I would reveal it to them myself, as soon as I became aware of what it really was. And my mind was filled with joy at the thought of how I would surprise them, and of how they should be surprised.

That strange knowledge lay like a warmth at my heart. It lit the dull night for me, so that through the gloom and mirk I walked as on air and in radiance. All that I had gone through vanished from my memory. It was as though it had never been. Nothing was any more but this new-found rest and contentment.

Happiness! I had found it at last; and it was more worth finding than anything I had yet experienced.

But the end of our walk was nigh. At a distance was the gleam of lights, and black silhouettes about them. We increased our pace, I, willingly enough, for I wished to tell them a secret; and in a short time we came to the great steps and mounted them. Men were there with torches, and we walked gaily from darkness into light.

Reaching the top, on the wide platform before the door, she turned to me with a smile, and she stopped dead. I saw the smile frozen on her face. I saw her face blanch to the whiteness of snow, and her eyes widen and fix and stare. She clasped her bosom with both hands and stood so, staring.

Then something, a self of me, detached itself from me, and stood forward and looked also.

I saw myself. My mouth was twisted sidewards in a jolly grin. My eyes were turned inwards in a comical squint, and my chin was all a sop of my own saliva.

I looked at myself so for a mortal moment, and I awakened.

DARLING

DARLING

I

OLD Four Eyes was quite young. That is, he was about thirty-three or four years of age, but there are people who are born middle-aged, and he was one of them: he was called "old" for that reason; and he was called "Four Eyes" because he wore spectacles.

He had attained to all the dignity which the average man can hope for, that is, he was married and he had a situation. In the latter he had reached the emolument beyond which the average man does not dare to covet; that is, he had thirty-five shillings a week.

He had married his wife very largely because there was no one else who could so easily be married; and she, after attending quite a respectable time, had married him because no one better had turned up.

It was not that any particular urgency of the blood drove them to each other's arms; for they could not have mustered one infantile passion between them. It was that one married at a certain time after leaving school. It is one of the things that are done. They lived on the same tram-line. They went to the same Church. They attended the same semi-clerical or lay clerical meetings and missions which every Church fosters. They were thus continually meeting, and at last saluting, and at long last, through the introduction of a clergyman, speaking.

He saw her home once: he saw her home again: then he always saw her home.

Why did they go to Church? It was not to praise God—they would not have known how to do such a thing. It was not to pray —their characters were not strong enough for such an exercise of intellect and will. They went to Church because they had gone there when they were children; because it was the proper thing to do; because Church and its accessories formed a Society in which they could mix, and which rescued them from the feeling of individuality and detachment which can so easily become a sense of utter loneliness and despair.

When two young people have convoyed each other home in the late hours they must do the right thing, that is, they must get married: and so these two got married.

Love! There was none of it. Even affection does not seem to be necessary for such a coupling. Of course, they had both read the right books, and from these had gleaned that love existed and that affection was a postulate for matrimony. To be loving was, therefore, the right thing to be, and they loved as in duty bound. They said "darling" to each other frequently, and, altho' less frequently, they clasped each other's hands.

They had a wedding party—they both saved up for it from their very meagre wages —and to the wedding a dozen people of their own tribe were invited, and were regaled on lemonade and buns: there were other and more notable meats than these. The proper speeches were made; the proper toasts were drained in bubbling and hissing glasses. Everything, they told each other afterwards, went off splendidly, and they went away to a seaside place for six days.

Then they returned to the small house they had taken and furnished on the instalment system, and thus they became man and wife, and the one flesh.

II

FOR a week or two they were almost excited. Their meals were no longer solitary. Each night they shared a supper and a bed. They walked arm in arm to Church twice every Sunday, and thus enlinked they walked back together and did not separate on arriving at a door.

When the morning tea was prepared, she would call out:

"Breakfast is ready, darling."

And when he was going to work he would say:

"Did you notice where I left my hat, darling?"

She did not go to work any more, for that was not the thing; and when he came home in the evening he listened dutifully to the conversation which she had accumulated during a companionless day.

Indeed, he sometimes thought she talked for longer than was necessary about the way the kitchen tap dripped. When it was turned off it did not entirely turn off.

At first he admired and envied her ease in speech; for he could not at all have uttered so many words about a water tap. He marvelled at her. Each night brought its own subject. It might be about the fading oilcloth on the hall: it might be about cockroaches in the basement: it might be that the silk in her wedding-present umbrella had slit. On these subjects, on all and every subject, she was able to emit unceasing and perfectly grammatical phrases.

He sat with her in the parlour and hearkened diligently to her tale. He would lie silent in bed, and, long after the candle had been blown out, he would stretch beside her in the darkness, and would listen, listen, listen.

He could not help listening, and the thin sound of his wife's voice began to beat on his ear as something monstrously dull, as an eternal, inexplicable, complaint.

He almost regretted having got married.

III

HE had a long-haired thin-grown moustache. He had a large badly cut nose. He had dull blue eyes which stared, as tho' he were listening with them instead of with his ears. He had as little chin as could be without having no chin at all. His ears swung slightly outwards. The ends of his trousers flopped about his ankles, and from the flop and waggle of these garments one knew that his legs were as skinny as matches. One divined that his elbows were sharp enough to wear a hole through his coat, and that his feet were longish and flattish and that his toes mounted energetically on top of each other.

One knew that he was less protected against life than a snail is. One knew that one could do anything one pleased to him without fear; and that, unless the thing done was terribly public, he would not even complain.

His wife knew it, but she had only blood enough for the little, bitter dislike which flowed from her in a thin, bitter, unceasing sound of words.

He liked everyone in the world. He liked everything in the world. He liked anything. That, if he had an ambition, was all his ambition, to be let like people; to be let placate people, and to let them see that he liked them.

Never was such a handshake as he gave. It seemed he would never again let go of one's fingers. Never did eyes beam on one with such entire assurance that here was goodwill. That here was one who would be gratified by your good fortune. That here was one who would laugh and perform antics like a dog if that would give you pleasure. That here was one who implored you not to do him harm.

IV

LIFE flowed on.

Three years of the slab of nonsense which he called life went by; and he was alive, a little bonier than before, but with an imperceptible growth of boniness that left him unchanged to himself.

He was more eager than ever when he clasped your hand in both of his own, and clung to it as thinking that here might be safety. On your approach he wagged his tail with a woeful energy; and his dumb eyes implored you to take him away with you, and feed him. To tie him up, if you had the heart to do that, but to take him away with you, and not let him stray any longer.

For he was terribly afraid. He had lost all hope, and he saw the end coming to him irresistible as death. He saw the calamity and disaster to which he was fated coming on him implacably, and he wanted to be let off: he wanted a corner where he could lay his bones on straw and blink at the sun.

For he was tired; and could no longer work as he used to work. His wife's voice, that unceasing, bitter little drone, came between him and his work: it drowned all his thoughts: it destroyed the mere mechanical remembrance which was his work. He could no longer be certain that his tots at the end of the ledger were right. He could not remember the thing which he had been told to remember for to-morrow; for she droned into his ear in the middle of the column of figures; and she buzzed at him while his superior was giving him instructions.

The other men began to play pranks on him.

They filled his ink bottle with lumps of blotting paper, so that when he lifted out the pen he would put a two-inch blot on the ledger. They stole his cup at the lunch hour and he found in its place a cup full of red ink. They turned his desk upside down: tore his papers, bashed in his hat; spread gum on his chair. They did everything to him which careless, malevolent minds could think of, knowing that as he did not know whom to complain of he would never complain.

Things began to get unbearable. Not unbearable for him; for until death came he could bear anything. Things began to get unbearable for his masters. They did not know who played the pranks, but they knew all about the pranks; and as his incompetence became more evident so their speech to him became more short, their looks more dissatisfied.

In the face of these things he could return and return, but he could not battle; he could oppose there nothing but his eagerness to please and his dumb eyes.

He saw his dismissal coming; and with it he saw the end of life, the fading away of the green earth, and the going out of the sun. He strove against his dismissal with humility, and further than his abjectness humility itself could not go.

It was a thing of shame; and God knows he was ashamed. It was obscene; and perhaps God counted his tears as they slid burning and tickling along that gaunt nose into his moustache.

V

He was dismissed, and he stood before his master as a sheep might stand before its butcher. He listened without a word and went away without a word.

His wife droned and droned and droned. But now it was not only in the night time; that dark cavern of thin, unintermitting sound. She had all the day to talk in and all the night; and both the day and the night were filled by her with words.

He fled from the house. He walked up streets and down streets; pushing open shop doors, office doors, and doors of stables and yards, seeking employment; carrying his frightened eyes and his humility into every sort of place and every kind of company.

But he might as fruitfully have asked for employment from the winds and the waters.

There was no employment for him on the earth. There was no place for him under the wide canopy of heaven.

The little money he had managed to save vanished away.

The people from whom he had hired his furniture came with a van and took it away again. His wife went away to live with a cousin until she could find work.

For a few days and nights he roved about the empty house; eating stale crusts that he found, drinking water from the tap, sleeping on the rubbish-littered floor. Then one morning the landlord knocked and asked for the keys. He gave them and the landlord saw him off the premises.

He was in the street, and he had nothing in the world but a pair of spectacles.

He stared through them at the clouds. He looked at the clouds fixedly as he paced forward, thinking that maybe he would see God through his spectacles.

THE WOLF

THE WOLF

I

ONE had but to look at his face to know that he was a quiet man. Indeed, he was the quietest man in the village. There were some who carried that modest statement further and maintained that he was the quietest man in the world; but these people, as we say, go beyond the beyonds.

He was tallish, without being tall; he was thinnish, without being skinny; he had pale blue eyes which seemed as though they had been glazed after they were put in; he had light fair hair that plastered itself down in the places where it could be seen, and stuck a surreptitious hair or so up in the places where they could not be seen. His feet turned inwards; not much it is true, but whatever turn might be to them was inwards; and although his knees did not knock together when he walked still they nearly knocked together. His ears were put on so unhandily that you might have sworn he put them on himself, and a glance told you that he was an unhandy man.

When you looked at him first you thought of a sheep; but on a second glance you racked your brains to think of some animal which was not quite so larky as a sheep. Does not a sheep carry itself with a certain timid dignity? And it has a robust curiosity to boot.

He did not seem to be married, but he was, and he had the right wife. The neighbours said so, afterwards, and the saying gave her a modified popularity.

Her sole claim to note before that had been that every time she came close enough to her husband's head she hit it. She hit it with anything that was handy—a potstick, a saucepan, her fist, anything.

It was not that she disliked her husband's head. It was more that she did not see it, or that she saw something which seemed to be eternally in her way. That she hit, and shooed out of doors as she would have shooed out an enterprising, unnecessary chicken.

When a chicken is hit it squawks and rustles and runs, a brief feathery uproar; but when he was struck he just went; he faded; he was gone.

His wife didn't know he had gone; she didn't know he had come; she didn't know she had hit him.

He was a quiet, quiet man.

That being so, one was the more stupefied when he was brought before the magistrates, and folk unerringly, unanimously, remembered the name of the animal they could not recall, when they said he was not exactly like a sheep, but that he was more like one of them . . . one of them what-do-you-call-thems.

"Hasn't he the look of a wolf?" said the people, "a wolf with softening of the brain?"

And everyone was satisfied, for they had a name on him at last.

They said, "Wait until he does his six months' hard and the wife gets a grip of him."

II

THERE was a fair at Carroll's Pass five miles away.

To get to Carroll's Pass from where he lived you turned to the east and walked straight in front of you through a narrow valley; a funnel of green bushes and grey rocks that zig-zagged between two long low-lying mountains.

His wife took him to the door of their cottage which was itself perched on the spike of a hill; turned him to the necessary direction, and said:

"Follow your nose until you come to Carroll's Pass."

She slung a crate of fowl on his shoulders and pushed him on the road, calling out:

"Half a crown the chicken and don't bring less, or——!"

He followed his nose.

People passed him, but they passed him the way one goes by a bush or rock, or a cow. He was almost as invisible as these quietudes are, and for the same reason; for who, having seen a cow twice, ever sees a cow again in life? The milkman! Not he, he milks something that he doesn't know is there; but a bull has to be warily met, warily passed, and he bears an uneasy, irresponsible hook beside each of his ears.

One sees a bull perpetually, and one even sees him in places where he is not. But a cow——!

He went down the rough slope; he trudged through the valley and he came to Carroll's Pass.

The world was there before him.

A world of squawks and squeals and grunts and cackles and shrill calls of women and great guffaws of men; with now and then the long lamentable uproar that is made by a donkey pealing above all other noises; and continually, the sharp and gruff and eager bark, yelp, howl, growl, and snarl of every kind of dog that you could put a name to.

At a little distance all these noises become one sound and it is as the sound of the sea.

He heard that sound, and he walked into it. It swallowed him up, and therein he disappeared from mortal eye for the space of six hours.

When he reappeared the sun was sinking in a red distance, the fair was all gone home again; there was a deep silence everywhere, and he was as drunk as a lord.

How had he managed it? It is a mystery. He had no longer a crate of chickens on his shoulders. He had no hat. He had no coat. His boots were laced to his feet, so he had them. His trousers were braced to his shoulders and were still his own.

He trod with a kind of cautious happiness into the track of the setting sun, and stood all in a glory of misty gold for a few minutes; then he pointed his nose due west and started for home.

He took two steps to the left, then two steps to the right, then he took one step in front—and then he halted again; readjusted his nose to the compass; spat on his hands, and had another try at it.

That was his progression, and by balancing

his nose on the wind he got forward half a mile in good shape.

He was in the green funnel that wound round between two hills.

Now and then he tried to kick out of his path a rock that was eight feet deep and twenty feet round; now and again he waved a bush from the road with the gesture of one who will be obeyed.

But he was cheerful, he was tolerant, and when these objects refused to budge he went round them and laughed at their discomfiture.

"They," he said, "would never think of going round me."

"Stupid!" said he to a tree, and he dodged it in almost the neatest way imaginable.

Midway in the green and grey funnel there was, for quite a distance on either side, a sudden flattening of the ground. The mountains had, as it were, taken two steps backwards and a narrow mile-long hollow lay between them. The path still ran through this hollow; and here, on either hand, it was bordered by a ditch, into which the hills drained themselves in the wet weather, and which was always moist even in the dry.

He came to this point and undertook the path; but he had the trouble of the world in circumventing the two ditches. They met him everywhere, and instead of being, as they should have been, on his right and left hand, they were continually, unaccountably, in front of him.

But he was cheerful; and each time that he found himself staring into a hole he nodded at it, turned away with a chuckle, balanced his nose on the wind that blew from the west, and won a pace forward.

III

DURING one of these adjustments, as he stared forward with his chin up, he became aware of the stir of life immediately in front of him; and on this movement he gazed with the gravity of one who understands movement and approves of it.

Two small children were playing on the path. They were prettily dressed, and at a glance one saw that they did not belong to the farmer or labouring class of the neighbourhood. At a distance in front up the hill to the right there was a neat cottage which was sometimes let in the summer months to those folks who have a strange but quickly satisfied liking for country air. There possibly they were at home for a week or two.

The children, a boy and a girl, were very young, perhaps six or seven years of age, and they were playing together. Their game was not in the least complicated. It could be followed by the haziest eye.

They stood each to one side of the road, and then they trotted past each other to the other side of the road. There was a curious, demure deliberation in their play; and there was a curious, demure silence between them.

He looked on these little ones, and his heart filled suddenly with tenderness; he smiled on them from afar, and then, recovering his balance, he moved in their direction.

Every few steps he stood and gazed and wagged a tender wag at the little ones; and the nearer he drew to them the tenderer he became; but they were intent on their game and did not observe him.

By dint of loving them he became aware that they also loved him; and, when only a small distance away, he lifted his voice in that belief and waved a friendly hand.

The children turned at once in his direction and stood at gaze.

He beckoned to them but they did not move; and the smallest, the most trifling, irritation stirred in his mind. He loved them and they did not run to him! What a singular thing that was. Well, he would go to them; and he at once set about it.

He took two steps to the right. Then he took two steps to the left. Then he took one step forward.

Without a word said, with one sole accord, the two children turned about and trotted down the road.

He was bewildered. He looked at those little legs trotting their demure trot, and it seemed to him that an injustice was being committed. He loved them, and they were running away from him!

He spat on his hands, and took himself to a dog trot after them.

A drunken man walks with great difficulty but he can run with no trouble at all. The quickened action gives him his balance, and the momentum he gets holds him in the balance and in the road. He caught up on the children in two minutes and gripped each of them in a hand that was easily large enough for those small shoulders.

But now he was standing, and his standing was uneasy. The little girl twisted from his hand and trotted forward again. He shook the little boy with loving violence. The girl trotted back to him, and with all the fury of a tigress but with only the weight of a butterfly, she beat her small fists against his thigh.

"Let out my brother, man," said she.

He twisted his head round to her, raised his hand, and, with all the irritation of a loving but vexed parent, he slapped her on the cheek. That slap sent the child backwards the width of the road and down into the dust.

He lost his balance, and to save it let go the boy's shoulder. He staggered, waved his arms round and round like the wings of a mill, and, with only half of a balance recaptured, he stared down into a hole.

He went inevitably, almost willingly, into the ditch; and, as he fell, the children, silent still, but with staring eyes, began again their demure little trot down the road.

He nodded gravely at the bottom of the ditch and he spoke gravely to it.

"I'll teach you," said he, "to run away from me."

Then he placed his cheek carefully on a large soft piece of mud and went peacefully to sleep.

THE BOSS

THE BOSS

I

To his desk in the secluded managerial room the entire vast business of his company flowed in departmental reports or suggestions; and that only could occur which had been authorised by his hasty initial.

He knew all that was happening, whether near at hand or far away. He knew why this department paid and why that other languished, or just paid for its keep. Why such an official should get an immediate increase in his salary and much personal affability; and why such another should be treated with brevity or reserve.

All the machinery of the great organisation was under his hands. He touched it at any point he pleased; and there was no part of it obscure or unimportant to his mind.

The business was prosperous when he took command, but it was his ambition that it should be marvellous; and that when the name of the place was uttered it should impact upon the mind of the hearer swiftly, monstrously, like a winged mountain, like an earthquake on wheels.

He required help for all this, but he would not have admitted a requirement in that term; for his predecessors in the caste had purged that kindly word from their vocabulary, and had translated it cleverly, atrociously, into the word "hands."

There is but one disposable material in the universe—it is life; and for man, when he has evolved beyond rudimentary abilities, there is but one tool to be found—and it is man. To the manager's mind man had become as common as mud; as useful as coal; as unvoiced and anonymous as either.

He would have preferred a true machine under his hand for he had no vendetta against his kind; but every machine is harnessed to a man; and a man is the motor, the crank, and the brake, however otherwise we distribute the names.

Here is one who is good-for-nothing

where he is; he must be put somewhere where his value can be used. Here is one from whom all value has been extracted; he must be thrown out. Thank heaven that he is a legged, a mobile affair, and will not remain where he is thrown as a tongued eyesore, a perpetual exasperation; and thank heaven for the police who keep the rubbish heaps moving on.

II

THE statement that the meek shall inherit the earth was profoundly uttered; for we come inevitably to the possession of that which we do not care to enjoy; but those who are capable of such careless surrender are not meek in the accepted term. Their values are different, and they cannot be bribed with earths for which they have no need, nor be disturbed by any impact of circumstance. Circumstance falls from them as water falls from a cliff; the world they move in, or that for which they are bound, is not visible to the eye of a manager, and in all relations they are free.

But there are meek people, poor people, cowards; and they are meek and poor and cowardly bcause they want urgently something or other. The man who has a desire is condemned to be a slave; and he shall have outgrown his desire before he attains it. But the like breeds the like, and he will find a new desire in time to prevent him losing the old fetter. He is obedient, and he is the backbone and prop of all tyrannies and systems of tyranny. On thy belly shalt thou go, and, God help us! our heads are full of bellies.

Did the manager cease to be a slave when he became a tyrant? or is there any difference between a tyrant and a slave?

Sometimes he had the trouble which he understood, and circumvented; but in almost all cases the oil of dismissal could smooth any troubled water; and after it there remained scarcely a ripple or wimple on the surface of the business.

He smoothed and smoothed endlessly; that is, he discharged ruthlessly every man who did not absolutely suit him. But all clockwork and interchangeable parts get tired and get rusty and stick; and there is no let to one's supervision.

Thus, in keeping the machine in order he became a tyrant not of cruelty but of efficiency; and was himself as much a slave to the system as any timid underling in the lower office. The donkeyman tending his engine does not recognise that he is the engine; and the Boss, overlooking, planning, combining; in an endless wakefulness of energy and readiness and sacrifice; overlooked all, and was obedient as a dog because he was known to himself, and was called by others, the Manager.

Yet he had a character; that is, an intellectual consciousness of his own being apart from his acts. He had a will, but it swirled into one narrow, habitual passage and there swept everything before it. He had a culture, that is an immediate perception, for other things are knowledge but this instancy is culture; so he saw a thing mentally; and on the very point and tipping of vision he saw business or not business, and proclaimed infallibly that it was or it was not "worth while."

III

THERE was a man, the head of a department, and the manager had his knife in this man. The man knew the knife was in, the whole office knew it; and he, the man, and the office, were waiting for the moment to arrive when the knife would get the twist they expected, and the man would disappear.

The man was a good man, in the sense of a tool, but he was not good enough. He put into the business all that he had, but he had not enough; and while his department was profitable it was not profitable in the figures which the manager demanded from it.

So this sub-manager was one who was treated first with decent reserve and then with the indecent brevity which is a business advertisement, that if the subject is a tactful person he will resign; and the cumulative effect of which forces almost any man to resign.

There is a business etiquette, and while the lower castes are discharged openly and casually the higher ones are permitted to retain their personal dignity and are allowed to discharge themselves.

But this man did not resign!

The manager gave the adept twist to the knife which he had seen practised so often and which he had practised so often himself; but the man did not resign; and the manager was nonplussed.

Here was a thing which, in his experience, had not happened before, and he pondered it. He not only twisted the knife, but, as the business saying is, he put the screw on. He might as fruitfully have put his hat on, for the man did not resign; and the manager saw himself confronted, not alone with disobedience, but with that terrifying form of it which consists in a denial of the rules of the game.

It is a rule of the game that the other person's pride must do one fair half of the evil which you meditate against him.

IV

THE manager looked at the man, not in person but in space; he surveyed him from the seclusion of the vast managerial apartment, and against that man his mind directed itself in an anger which steadily became a hate.

When they had to meet he contrived that their meeting should be public; and if his remarks were few they were loud; and his departure was calculatedly abrupt.

When, not having special reason to meet the man, he did meet him, this also he arranged should be in public; but on these meetings he did not see the man; he overlooked him, or looked through him as though he were woven of empty air and was not visible.

The former of such meetings was taken as

the twist of the knife; the second was understood as the putting on of the screw, and neither of them worked. For the man grew affable as the manager grew distant; and presented an unexpressive unconscious back to the eye which had arranged to look at him and through him as though he were a ghost or a plate-glass window.

Yet if a thing had to be done the manager was not one to shrink from it. He had obeyed the rule and had given his man the equitable opportunity of saving his dignity which the rule prescribed.

He determined to dismiss the department manager, and he knew that it would be a pleasure to look into that face as he uttered the formula which he was carefully meditating.

It would be brief, the formula; but it would be as expressive as the snarl of a dog. There should be no obscurity in the bullet of a sentence he intended to fire; for, he considered it almost with terror, if the meaning was not adequately and irrevocably conveyed, that man would have it in him to return to his work and to overlook the dismissal.

He thought for a moment of discharging him in public and he would have done so willingly but that it would be bad for the staff morale, and might seem, that which business affairs must never appear, personal. It was personal, however, for between the pair there existed a relation which, although it was formed entirely of dislike, was palpitatingly real.

The knowledge that the manager has a personal side must not emerge in business; for while a business will court advertisement with all its heart it will avoid publicity with all its soul; and the great, domestic asset of a manager, a general, a professor, is his anonymity. That must be preserved or anything may result; anything, unless we are prepared to make the largest possible assumption and declare that a great man occupies the position.

The reason he did not write to him, with the dismissal instant in black and white, and immortalised by copying into a letter-book was, that he wished to look into the man's face, and deliver himself into that face like a thrust sword.

He determined to see the man and to

dismiss him by word of mouth, and he determined to write to him also in such chosen
and cogent terms that even he should find
no back-door to them.

V

HE touched a bell and told the messenger to inform the manager Department C that the Manager wished to speak to him.

He stood for a moment looking about the room; then he moved two chairs which were near his desk to the side of the room; and he manipulated a third chair into a position which he carefully chose.

The man knocked at the door, entered, and was invited by the manager's expressive hand to the not too distant but very detached chair referred to.

The distance between this chair and the manager's desk permitted conversation, but it prohibited familiarity; and it had the effect of isolating the individual who sat on it not only from the manager's desk but almost from the room. He was marooned on it.

He was segregated and indicated by it as a stranger.

The person who occupies a seat thus cleverly arranged feels, though it be insensibly, that he has lost all contacts; that he is "in the air"; and his disadvantages become so immediately evident to himself that the equilibrium of his mind is disturbed and an automatic idea of inferiority awakens in him, with its logical sentiment of humility and obedience.

But the manager had misread his man; or had, from a feeling of antagonism and egotism, neglected to accord him the personal mental interest which had already been emotionally incurred.

The man had come in silently. He sat down silently, grimly; posing with slow care across his knees an immaculate hat and a long, flexible whalebone which could be described as a walking-stick.

He was not distressed by the isolated chair; he was too self-centred, self-contained, self-conscious for any such tricky distresses to reach him. He looked on the manager very calmly, with a certain weight of regard as tho' his whole head was bent upon him and not his eyes alone; and at him the manager looked, with no weight, but with eagle directness.

If one may compare essentially different things, and small things to great, there was the difference between their gaze that there is between a block of granite and a flash of lightning. The one could topple smashingly, the other plunge as disastrously; and from both, in both, there was tranquillity and power.

Two minds were made up, and they were immovable. Each as he looked, felt the other; and each knew that here was determination and carelessness.

VI

THE manager spoke:

"The condition of your department is not satisfactory."

The man nodded the large head, which was directed as an eye upon the manager.

"And," the latter continued, "I have invited you here in order that you may tender me your resignation."

"I shall not resign," said the immovable head.

"You will place me under an awkward— unpleasant necessity."

"What you meditate is neither awkward nor unpleasant," said the man.

He rose from his chair; a powerful bulk of movement; and strode to the door. There was a bolt inside the door and he shot this. He returned to his chair and bent his head profoundly on the manager.

"Let us understand each other," said he.

The manager stood from his chair.

"Open that door," he commanded.

"In a moment," said the immovable man, "when I have said what I came to say."

He lifted his chair out of isolation; placed it nearer to the manager's desk, and sat upon it. Then he put on his hat; not impertinently, but obviously to leave his hands free.

The manager sank back into his own chair, and regarded his finger nails.

"Nothing that you can say," said he, "will alter my determination in this matter."

"I am aware of that," the other replied, "but I also am determined to say what I have come to say; you have not all the determination of the world."

The manager nodded.

Said the other:

"I am in this fortunate position, that I do not depend on my employment for my livelihood."

The manager raised and lowered his brows in the manner of one who ticks off items which he fears will be lengthy, but will, of necessity, have some conclusion.

His companion continued:

'I am thus so free that I can afford to resent ill-will, and chastise a personal antagonist."

The manager wearily checked this statement and permitted it to disappear.

"Between you, the six months' manager of this house, and I, who had held an important position here for ten years, there has arisen a personal ill-will, and you are the aggressor. You have determined to place on me a public affront, I have determined to resent it and to punish it."

The manager nodded another item away.

"In what way," said he, "am I to be punished?"

"You have called me here to discharge me. I," touching his whalebone, "have brought this here to beat you."

"You understand," said the manager, "what will happen after you have beaten me."

"I shall pay the fine or do the three months. It is a matter of indifference to me."

"In that case," said the manager, "I take this opportunity of informing you that this establishment has no further need of your services."

[196]

VII

THE two men looked with cold excitement, with cold rage, at each other. The man eased the whalebone in his hand, rose to his feet, and strode to the desk.

"I think I can manage to do you three months' damage before they break the door open," said he.

He reached a hand to the manager's shoulder; and the latter's hand stretched automatically forward and hovered over the bell upon his table. Thus they halted for two seconds staring fixedly at each other. Then, with a disdainful movement of the lips, the manager removed his hand without having touched the bell; and at once the man took his hand from the manager's shoulder.

As instant as had been their movements so quickly had all anger evaporated from the discharged man's mind; and where rage had been there remained pride. He was not proud of himself, nor was he proud of the manager; in a curious but satisfactory way he was proud of man; and he was extraordinarily happy.

"You did not ring the bell," said he with a smile. And by that smile the manager's mind was emptied of hate or disdain as if something magical had come and these had not dared to await it.

"No," he replied, "this seemed rather a personal matter."

The man turned to the door.

"Well I must be off."

"I am to take it," said the manager, "that you tender your resignation."

"Pooh," said the man, "you sacked me a minute ago, good-bye."

"Good-bye," said the manager, and the door closed between them.

He sat down, and for a time laughed quietly to himself. But the remainder of the day passed for him in a lassitude which he could not account for, and could not quite shake off.

In a week the matter was only remembered

as a curious episode; in a month it was forgotten, and he had sacked two other men.
Yet when six months had elapsed he had not
discharged anyone else; and thereafter he
rarely dismissed any.

But two years passed before he resigned
a position in which he took no further interest, and in which, he considered, he was
leading the life of a donkey.

THE END

Date Due